EVERYTHING IS EPIC: STORIES

EVERYTHING IS EPIC

Stories

MICHAEL C. KEITH

SILVER BIRCH PRESS
LOS ANGELES, CALIFORNIA

ISBN-13: 978-0615795621

ISBN-10: 0615795625

Book and Cover Design: Silver Birch Press

Cover Photo: "Parachute Jump, Coney Island" by littleny

Published by Silver Birch Press, Los Angeles, California

Web: Silverbirchpress.com

Contact: silverbirchpress@yahoo.com

4

AUTHOR'S NOTE

The stories in this volume first appeared in the following publications: *Fiction on the Web, Bleeding Ink Anthology, Static Movement, Clever Magazine, Black Lantern, Lowestoft Chronicle, Greensilk Journal, Whiskey Paper, Connotation Press, Quail Bell Magazine, Underground Voices, Surreal Grotesque, Smokebox Magazine, and Blue Hour Magazine.*

I continue to be in the debt of Susanne Riette, Nicki Sahlin, and Christopher Sterling for their generous comments and cogent suggests during the draft stage of these stories. A writer could not have better literary guardians.

ALSO BY MICHAEL C. KEITH

Sad Boy

Of Night and Light

Hoag's Object

And Through the Trembling Air

Life is Falling Sideways

Norman Corwin's 'One World Flight' (with Mary Ann Watson)

The Radio Station

Sounds of Change (with Christopher Sterling)

Radio Cultures

The Quieted Voice (with Robert Hilliard)

The Next Better Place

Dirty Discourse (with Robert Hilliard)

The Broadcast Century (with Robert Hilliard)

Queer Airwaves (with Phylis Johnson)

Talking Radio

Waves of Rancor (with Robert Hilliard)

Voices in the Purple Haze

The Hidden Screen (with Robert Hilliard)

Signals in the Air

Radio Programming

Global Broadcasting Systems (with Robert Hilliard)

Radio Production

Selling Radio Direct

Broadcast Voice Performance

CONTENTS

EVERYTHING IS EPIC

Follow'd then

A classic lecture, rich in sentiment,

With scraps of thunderous Epic

— **LORD TENNYSON**

If you believe in me, I'll believe in you.

—LEWIS CARROLL

EVERYTHING IS EPIC

"For heaven's sake, Walter, it's *not* a blizzard! There's only a dusting of snow on the ground, and the weatherman says we'll only get a couple of inches. You always make a mountain out of a molehill. Lord, how you go on."

"Oh, be quiet!" Walter blurted, angry that she was making him feel like the boy who cried wolf, again.

For most of their long marriage, Walter Faraday had experienced similar accusations from his wife, Clare. As a result he regarded his spouse as a radical minimalist. To him, she had a zealot's passion to downsize things—"We *haven't* done that a hundred times," "It's not *that* expensive," "The car isn't *that* old," "You're not *that* sick," "It isn't *that* far..."

Walter knew he had a tendency to exaggerate, and he recognized it as a family trait. Indeed, both his sisters and mother loved to put a grandiose spin on things, and he viscerally disliked it when they did so. But he was who he was, and he couldn't abide by his wife's constant carping about his tendency to embellish events. It seemed innocent enough to him—certainly undeserving of his wife's unending denunciations. Her digs were hurtful and embarrassing, especially when they were around friends.

One evening after the couple had had another particularly heated exchange about his habit of elaborating on the facts, he stood alone in the kitchen gazing out of the window attempting to calm himself. *She's such a damn pain. Won't give a frigging inch. Makes everything I say sound foolish,* he thought.

As he stood lamenting the situation, he suddenly noticed something very strange in his backyard. An exceptionally bright object was floating in the air only a few feet from the house. When he leaned closer to the window, it appeared to shoot directly skyward and vanish. *Holy crap! A UFO? Yes, a UFO. What else could it be?* reflected Walter.

After a moment, he ventured outside to investigate what he was sure he'd seen. As he looked up into the early evening sky, he thought he saw the same strange object spinning off into the distance. *Why our backyard? Were we being observed by an extra-terrestrial life form?* he wondered. The idea filled him with apprehension, but he decided not to reveal the experience to his wife. *She'll just think I'm overstating again.* You're such a drama queen, *she'll say. To heck with that! Not going there.*

It took Walter longer than usual to get to sleep that night, because he could not excise the backyard scene from his head. By dawn he was up and peeking out of the kitchen window to where he'd seen the mysterious object hovering. He detected a discoloration on the lawn in that exact location. *The grass is burnt! It happened! It really happened! They'll be back, I bet.*

Over breakfast with Clare, he wrestled with the urge to tell her about what had happened. But he remained silent about it until she headed to the door leading outside.

"What are you doing?"

"Going to water the flowers. Why?"

"You won't believe this, but I think it might not be a good idea to go out there."

"Huh? What are you talking about?"

"I saw something out there last night. I think it was an alien ship. It was just hanging there in the air."

"*What* the...? Wow, your imagination has *really* taken over."

"Look, I'm not making this up. I'm telling you what I saw," protested Walter.

"You're always seeing something beyond what actually exists. Everything is so *epic* with you, Walter," growled Clare, going to the door

Walter watched out the window as she moved to the spot above which the curious object had dangled the evening before. Suddenly a blinding flash filled the scene before him. When it dissipated, his wife was gone.

But there's nothing to equal, from what I hear tell,
that moment of mystery.— **GEORGE ELIOT**

EVER READY

My father fiddles with the on/off switch on his flashlight.

"Crap!" he grumbles and taps it against the palm of his hand. "Damn batteries are new, too."

The flashlight flickers on and his face lights up. "Good!"

He owns several flashlights. There is one within arm's reach everywhere in his house. He's always had lots of them. They're very important to him, and I've never been sure why.

"What are you looking for?" I ask him as he casts the flashlight's beam out of his bedroom window for at least the thousandth time.

"Just checking to make sure it works."

It's his standard answer to a question I've been asking him since I was a kid.

"You're always checking them, dad. How come?" I ask reflexively.

"The batteries die. Sometimes really soon, too, so you got to check them pretty often."

"But you do constantly."

"You can never check them enough, because when you need them, they damn sure better work."

"A jealous husband after you?" I joke, and my father ignores me—he's heard *that* line before.

When I was a kid, I was convinced that gangsters were tracking him down. Maybe he had crossed them and they wanted to come break his legs. When I told him my theory, he said that was ridiculous. I wasn't convinced, and the question of why he spent so much time shinning his flashlight into the night continued to intrigue, if not haunt, me.

"It's pretty weird doing that. A really strange habit," I remark.

"You don't know anything," he snaps—and I've heard that line before, too.

"Dad, c'mon. I'm going to head back to my apartment. Walk me to the door."

"Hold on!" he says, shushing me.

"What?" I ask, and he waves me to the window.

He has something in the beam of his flashlight. When it moves, the air empties out of my lungs.

"Jesus! What the…?"

"No problem," he says, holding the beam steady on the most hideous creature I have ever seen.

And then suddenly the grotesquery vanishes, almost as if it's been struck by a ray gun.

"There," says my father, turning to me with a look of triumph.

I steady myself against the wall and try to regain my breath.

"That's why I always check the batteries," he says.

And all the air a solemn stillness holds.

— THOMAS GRAY

OUT ON A LIMB

The house was in total darkness when Elvin Kells climbed from his bed to empty his bladder. The electric clock on his bureau did not display its luminous numbers and the streetlight outside failed to cast its usual soft glow inside to help him navigate his way to the bathroom.

Another power outage, thought Elvin, moving cautiously around the king size bed and past his wife's bulky wardrobe. His irascible prostate had recently forced him to sit while urinating since it was often a long, if not arduous, process. After several minutes, he returned to bed hoping the lights would be restored when he rose at five A.M. to ready himself for the long commute to work. He did not relish the idea of showering and dressing in the dark, and the thought of hitting the road without his morning cup of coffee was disagreeable in the extreme.

A loud thud awoke him with a start. For a moment he was disoriented having been torn from a dream that had him scaling the side of a steep cliff, something he would never do in real life. He looked closely at the clock and just barely discerned the outline of the digits 3:27.

"Damn, still no power," he muttered, recalling his earlier trip to the bathroom in complete darkness.

Elvin pressed the light button on his watch and discovered he had overslept.

"Crap!" he blurted, causing his wife, Cela, to stir and mumble something incomprehensible. "Go to sleep, honey," he whispered, patting her arm as he slipped from bed.

Elvin fumbled around in his closet with a flashlight and cobbled together an outfit for the day. He quickly dressed deciding against showering in the dark. He also decided to forego shaving as well. *So I look a little grubby for once*, he thought, as he scribbled a note for his sleeping wife: *Power is out. Call utility company. Love, E. XOX*

He was just a couple feet out of the front door when he noticed that several fallen tree limbs blocked the driveway. Another was pressed against the side of the house, prompting him to recall the loud noise that had startled him from sleep.

"Great, just what I need," he growled.

As he surveyed the situation, he saw wires snaking across the hood of his car and realized they were probably hot.

Touch it and you're fried, he thought, cringing at the image. The streetlamps were out, and he couldn't see nearby houses, so he couldn't tell if his neighbors were in a similar predicament. Elvin reached into his pocket for his cell phone. The screen lit up but showed there was no service.

"What the hell," he grumbled, discovering there was no Internet either.

His wife had heard him stumbling around the house and came downstairs to see what was going on.

"Where's the lights?" she asked, groggily.

"They're out. Trees fell on the power lines, or at least their branches did. I can't get anything thing on my iPhone either," reported Elvin.

"Are you going to work?"

"The driveway's blocked, so I can't get out," replied Elvin, still fiddling with his cell phone.

"Was there a storm last night? I didn't hear anything," offered Cela.

"You could sleep through a typhoon. I heard something hit the house, but that was after I noticed the power was out. It woke me up."

"What about Keri and Jim across the street? Do they have power?"

"I doubt it. I didn't see any lights in their house. Of course, they're probably not up yet, and I can't go over and check because there are live wires on the ground."

"Well, what are we going to do?"

"Let's listen to the battery radio to see what's going on," suggested Elvin.

To his surprise, the two stations he normally tuned were off the air.

"Jeez, that's weird," he murmured, as Cela looked on curiously.

Finally, a station known for its hip-hop music came in loud and clear, but instead of its usual hit rhythms it was full of urgent talk.

"It now appears that every part of the city is without power, and reports are coming in that surrounding areas are also experiencing a blackout..."

"How freaky is that?" muttered Elvin.

"What about mother? She's all alone, and I was supposed to take her to the doctor's today," commented Cela, apprehensively. "I better call her."

"There's *no* cell service," reminded Elvin.

"Oh, God. What are we going to do?"

"When it gets light, I'll go over to her house. I'll take the bike. The cars are blocked by the fallen tree limbs."

A sudden knock on the door startled them.

"You guys in there?" called their next-door neighbor, Len Benoit.

"Yeah, come in. The door's open," replied Elvin.

The Kells were not close with the Benoits, despite the proximity of their houses. On a couple of occasions, Cela attempted to befriend Betsy Benoit, but she was unresponsive to her overtures. So their connection with their closest neighbors amounted to an occasional wave when they spied one another in their respective yards.

"You see what's out there?" said Len, breathlessly. "Looks like a tornado hit. Power wires all over the place too. One is on your car."

"Yeah, I know. Guess it's like this all around here and in the city, too. The radio says other places are like this, and they don't know what caused it."

"Betsy is still sleeping. I didn't want to wake her figuring the lights would come back on soon. Then I went outside to get the paper, but my driveway is like yours, all cluttered with branches. I looked down the street as far as I could, and it's the same everywhere."

"It's starting to get light," observed Elvin. "We'll be able to tell how bad it is soon."

Cela, who had been listening to the radio, interrupted them.

"Did you hear that? They say it's like this all over the country. Almost every place is without power because tree limbs have taken down all the electrical lines."

"Holy, shit! That's insane," blurted Len. "Sorry, excuse my language. I better go tell Betsy. This sounds like a major crisis."

"Sure seems that way," responded Elvin, walking Len out of the house.

The dim morning light made it possible for both men to get a fuller sense of the destruction in their immediate area. Fallen tree limbs had crashed into houses and struck cars with devastating effect. Yards and driveways were cluttered with severed boughs and sprigs. Utility poles leaned at tenuous angles as large branches pushed down on the cables that connected them.

"It looks like…" mumbled Len, unable to find the words to describe the scene of devastation.

"Like nature has declared war on us," offered Elvin.

By late morning, the batteries in the Kells' radio were spent, and he replaced them from the stash he kept in the hall pantry.

"Damn, we got tons of A, AA, and Cs, but these are the last of the Ds. I should have bought one of those Red Cross wind-up radios. I almost did, too," reported Elvin.

The news had become more upsetting with each passing hour. Nothing was functioning, according to the latest reports. Airports were closed and hospitals were running on emergency power. Looting was reported at stores that stocked generators and other energy supplies. Again, Elvin lamented his lack of foresight.

"I was going to buy a generator after the last storm, but of course I didn't."

"Stop beating yourself up, honey. No one could have imagined anything like this," counseled Cela.

"I'll go to your mother's now, okay? Don't keep the radio on. We'll have to spare the batteries. Maybe I'll find some at one of the stores I pass," said Elvin, heading out to the garage.

"Be careful. Watch the downed wires. Tell mama we'll check in on her everyday. I know she has plenty of food and medicine. She's such a pack rat. We'll probably end up borrowing things from her."

"Not likely. You're your mother's daughter," said Elvin, putting put on his helmet and mounting his bike. "I'll be fine. You stay put. I should be back in a couple of hours."

The collapsed tree limbs limited how much Elvin could ride his bicycle. The streets were mostly blocked and clearings were few and far between. A public works vehicle at the end of his street was attempting to remove a giant branch. It occurred to Elvin that at the rate they were progressing, it would take months before things would be back to normal. Once he got to the mostly treeless main thoroughfare, he was able to ride unimpeded for several blocks, but when he turned onto his mother-in-law's street, he had to abandon riding and clamber over several downed branches.

It took him a quarter-of-an-hour to reach Janet Furlong's house and he felt spent. The tree branches that had dropped onto the elderly woman's street far outnumbered those on his. The once beautifully shaded lane reminded him of photos around Mount St. Helen's after it erupted. *Thorough devastation*, thought Elvin, surveying the destruction. Most of the modest homes on the street had been struck hard by the falling trees and not a single vehicle was spared. His mother-in-law's house seemed the single exception. Since the only trees on the property were in back, it appeared unscathed.

He knocked on the front door several times but received no response. It was possible she had gone to a neighbor's, figured Elvin, but he quickly dismissed the idea since she was barely mobile and certainly could not maneuver past the obstacles on the street.

Elvin called her name several times and then fished her house key out of the planter on the porch. It had been placed there for the very reason he now used it. Janet had hidden the key there in the event she was not able to get to the door and was unresponsive to calls. Cela had told her not to put it in such an obvious place, but her mother ignored her advice, claiming the neighborhood was crime-free and perfectly safe.

"No place is perfectly safe, mother," Cela had objected, but to no avail.

At first Elvin could not turn the key in its lock, and he wondered if Janet had installed a new one and forgotten to replace the old key. She had become forgetful in the last year, so it seemed possible, if not likely.

"Jesus," Elvin grumbled in frustration, giving the key a hard push.

The door flew open suddenly, nearly causing Elvin to fall inside the dark foyer.

"Janet, are you there?" he called. "It's Elvin."

After a quick search of the first floor, he made his way upstairs. The doors to the various rooms were shut as they always were, and Elvin went directly to his mother-in-law's bedroom that faced the backyard.

"Janet, it's Elvin. Are you in there?" he called, and receiving no answer, he opened the door.

A frightening sight greeted him. A long tree limb had crashed through the window and landed on the old woman, crushing her body as she lay atop her bed. Two sprigs had perforated her eyes creating the illusion that they were growing from her head. The sight repulsed Elvin and he ran from the room and out of the house. He sat on the front steps until his queasiness faded. When he caught sight of a person emerging from the house across the street, he shouted for help.

"Sorry, I got my own problems here," replied the man, who quickly disappeared from view.

"Thanks, I'll do the same for you some day!" shouted Elvin, perturbed.

He scanned the surroundings for anyone else that might assist him but saw no one. He then returned to where he had left his bicycle. In the process he nearly stepped on a downed power line. The realization that he had nearly been electrocuted shook him. *This can't be happening,* he repeated to himself, as he more carefully scanned the path before him to make certain no other wires awaited a careless misstep.

He was relieved to see the bicycle was right where he had left it. He retraced his earlier route hoping to encounter a police car or ambulance to report his mother-in-law's death. A few minutes into his ride, he spotted a cop and was able to flag him down. The response he received to his report was more than mildly upsetting.

"There's dozens reported dead and injured around here. Give me her address, and I'll add it to the list, mister."

After the police cruiser drove slowly away, Elvin continued his homeward direction. He had made up his mind not to tell Cela about her mother's death. He'd say she wasn't home. That she was probably taken to a friend's house. He figured Cela would intuit the fact soon enough after hearing about the widespread toll on human life. The longer she didn't know the truth the better, he thought.

Although he believed finding batteries was at best a remote possibility, he decided to check the two convenience stores on his route home. The first one had already been boarded up, and when he approached the second, he noticed several people scurrying away from it with objects in their arms.

"They're looting the place," Elvin mumbled, as he pulled into its parking lot.

He hid his bicycle behind a dumpster and ventured inside as several more individuals dashed past him clutching items.

"Dammit," grumbled Elvin, finding the battery rack empty.

Nearly all the shelves in the store were bare, and Elvin left now feeling both discouraged and angry. His dark mood deepened further when he discovered his bike missing.

"Son of a bitch!" he shouted, giving the dumpster a hard kick, which he regretted because of the pain it caused him on his walk home.

✂

Cela was standing in the doorway when he finally reached his house.

"What took you so long? I was worried."

"Someone stole my bike at the Store 24," replied Elvin, embracing his wife.

"What happened? Who…?"

"I tried to get batteries, but the place was full of looters and nothing was left. When I came out, it was gone. It's crazy out there. Like when Katrina hit New Orleans," explained Elvin.

"How's mama?"

"She wasn't at her house. I think she's probably at a friend's or neighbor's place."

"Maybe at Helen's or even Bev's. Did you check?"

"Sorry, no. It was hard going out there, and I wanted to try to get batteries. I'm sure she's fine, honey. I'll go check again when they've cleared some of the trees. It's practically impassible wherever you go and dangerous, too, with all the downed power lines. Almost stepped on one."

"I've been listening to the reports. Every place is affected. The whole country is closed down. The only places that have electricity are areas that had no trees. They're not sure why all the trees have suddenly lost their limbs. It's the strangest thing that ever happened and some experts believe that it's going to have an impact on oxygen levels pretty soon. Oh, Elvin, what's going to happen to us?" said Cela, panicking.

It was at that moment that Elvin was thankful they never had children, although there had been a time they wanted them very much. Now it was a responsibility he was glad to be spared.

"Things will be okay," responded Elvin, although wondering if they really would be.

By early afternoon, several of the street's residents had gathered at the Kells' and all seemed equally dazed by the crisis and fearful about its outcome. Two neighbors had generators and offered to provide hot water and cooked food to those who wanted them. Elvin was impressed by how people who hardly knew one another came together during disasters, at least early on. *Of course, when things deteriorate, a siege mentality will take over, and then it will be every man for himself,* he thought, recalling all the disaster movies he had ever seen.

"It's a good thing it's summer. At least, we won't freeze to death," offered Hank Gilbert, who lived a few houses down from the Kells'.

"Yeah, and there's plenty of fire wood laying around when it does get cold," added Carla Gilbert, with a smirk.

As the day waned, the residents of Clearview Drive agreed to gather at the Kells' house the next morning to further commiserate and listen to the President's planned address on the disaster.

"Does anybody have a supply of D batteries?" asked Elvin, as his neighbors departed.

"I got a few," answered Hank.

"A few? He's mister survivalist. He has more batteries than Eveready," his wife snickered.

"Hey, not such a stupid thing now, right?" replied Hank.

"Not at all," responded Elvin. "We should all be like you."

❊

What the President had to say put a quick damper on what had almost been a party-like atmosphere as people gathered the next morning in the Kells' kitchen. Things were far worse than anyone had imagined. An occasional "Oh my God!" from someone punctuated the Commander-in-Chief's dire statements.

The great Amazon and Boreal forests are decimated and as this satellite photo shows the rivers flowing through them have vanished, due to the incalculable number of fallen tree limbs now clogging them. Just what caused this unprecedented event is unknown. At this early stage in their investigation, experts indicate that the world's trees were not suffering from any known natural causes, such as Verticillium Wilt, Canker, Black Knot, or Fusiform rust. But, the fact is something has attacked the joints of the planet's conifers, deciduous, and palm trees, and the result of this historic phenomenon is far-reaching. Scientists speculate the cause may be the result of industrial pollution. Military reserves have been activated to aid in the clean up. Meanwhile, FEMA is making temporary housing available to those who have lost their homes...

"This is a nightmare," whimpered Sara Crosley, who lived the farthest from the Kells but had become acquainted with Cela through their mutual participation in yoga at the local YMCA.

"He said it's the worst natural disaster since the Ice Age," added Betsy, her eyes widening.

"Sounds like we're in deep doo-doo," replied Hank.

"Up to our ass, I'd say," observed Ken Logan, a widower who lived in the house diagonally across from the Kells.

"I think what the president says is bull," declared Len. "How the hell do all the trees in the world die simultaneously? That's crap. Must be an act of God or some freaking extraterrestrials."

"But why would God do such a thing?" inquired Betsy.

"Well, it sure as hell wasn't nature. That's not the way it operates," snapped Len.

The president's address continued for another half-hour and concluded with a plea to all citizens to assist in whatever way they could to help those in need and to aid local authorities in the vast clean up effort.

"What say we clear the block ourselves," suggested Hank. "If we wait for the town to do it, we could be trapped here for weeks."

His idea was met with unanimous approval, and for the remainder of the day, the residents of Clearview Drive hacked away at the mounds of debris clearing driveways and the street. By the third day of their shared efforts, they had succeeded in removing the obstructions to Mayfield Avenue, one of the town's primary thoroughfares. Thankfully, the town had cleared most of what had clogged that street. The Kells and their neighbors now had access to several areas of commerce, although the overwhelming majority of the retailers in the local shopping centers remained closed.

"It's nice that we can drive somewhere, but there's no place to go," lamented Cela. "It's like a ghost town out there."

✂

The Kells sat in the candlelight of their kitchen listening to the news on their portable radio. The reports centered on the President's several talks over the last few days in which the country was further informed of the gravity of the situation. Only a few regions of the country had electricity, and they were situated mostly in treeless places, such as the desert and plain states.

"Maybe we should go to Vegas. They say they still have power. It would be good to get away," offered Cela.

"We'd never get there. The airlines aren't operating and most of the roads between here and Nevada are still impassible. Besides, getting gas would be a problem, since stations are pretty much closed everywhere," replied Elvin, fiddling with the radio dial. "Damn, we're losing more signals. Only a couple stations still on the air."

"Is this it?' moaned Cela. "So we're prisoners here? The President says it's the same overseas and that there's really no timeline as to when things are going to get better. So many dead, and I'm worried about mother."

The Kells had traveled to Janet's street with the intention of looking for her. Due to Cela's recent knee surgery, she was unable to climb through the piles of tree limbs that blocked access to her mother's house. Elvin was thankful for that believing the death of Cela's mother would send her over the edge. While Cela waited in the car, he pretended to search for her mother. When he returned, he told her he had checked everywhere but had not found her. Uncertainty about her mother's welfare heightened Cela's anxiety, and for several hours she barely spoke.

✄

The next morning as neighbors congregated at the Kells as planned to listen to the President's daily address on the crisis, Cela saw that the group was slowly shrinking.

"I saw Keri and Jim pull out of their driveway late last night before I turned in. Their car isn't there this morning," said Hank.

"Where's Sara?" asked his wife. "She wasn't here yesterday either. Maybe we should check on her."

"Good idea," replied Elvin. "I'll go over to her place later."

At nine o'clock the President began what had become a daily address. What he had to say was far more disturbing than his previous announcements.

This morning I have the difficult duty to inform my fellow citizens that the crisis has taken a grave turn. EPA Director Don Hansen has informed the White House that oxygen levels are, indeed, declining and CO_2 levels are increasing as the apparent consequence of the *loss of the country's forests and trees. Foreign environmental agencies have made similar determinations. We are not sure what this means in the long term or if the Earth's air supply will deplete entirely. We do suggest that individuals with existing respiratory problems consult their physicians as soon as possible...*

Cela turned off the radio unable to listen any further.

"My God, we're all going to suffocate!" she blurted.

The Kells' neighbors stood in horrified silence.

"We don't know that," replied Elvin. "The President said they're not sure if the oxygen is going to be completely gone."

"I was wondering why I've been having more trouble breathing than usual with my 'asthma," remarked Len, who signaled to his wife to leave.

The rest of the group left the Kells' house saying little as the President's bombshell sank in.

When they were alone, Cela and Elvin sat silently at the kitchen table for several minutes until Cela insisted they go looking for her mother again.

"She's not there, honey," replied Elvin, not wanting to go through the subterfuge again.

"Maybe she's back," insisted Cela.

"I'm sure she's safe somewhere. We have to conserve on gas, because God knows when we'll be able to get any. I'm going to check on your friend, Sara. Want to take a walk?"

"No, I want to find my mother," objected Cela.

"Maybe later," said Elvin, rising to leave. "I'll be back soon."

It looks like a forest of telephone poles, Elvin mused, as he headed toward Sara's house. The block where she lived had not been cleared of limbs, but a narrow path down the length of it had been created. *An adorable yellow Cape with green shutters and flower boxes* was how Cela had described Sara's house and he spotted it instantly. It stood in stark contrast to the uniformly bland houses surrounding it. Erin knocked several times but there was no reply. As he was about to leave, the door opened a crack.

"Sara?"

"Is that you, Elvis?" giggled a soft voice.

"Elvin. It's Elvin, Sara."

"I know. I'm just kidding," said Sara, opening the door fully. "Sorry, I'm still in my robe. No place to go, so why dress, right?"

Sara stood before him in a flimsy satin bathrobe.

"We were wondering if you were all right. You haven't shown up for a couple days," said Elvin, realizing Sara's robe was little more than a negligee.

"I'm okay," she said with a slur. "I'm better than okay, in fact."

"Well, I'm glad to hear that. Hope you can come by our place tomorrow to hear the president," said Elvin, backing away from the entrance.

"Wait, come in. I could use some company. It's so damn quiet around here."

"Well, I really..."

"Come on. Just for a little while. I'm not going to bite you...I don't think," chuckled Sara, extending her arm toward Elvin.

"Okay, for a few minutes. Then I got to get back home."

Sara took his arm and guided him into her living room. "Sorry about the mess. Don't feel much like housekeeping since it's the end of the world and all," she chortled. Several empty liquor bottles were strewn across the carpeted floor and dirty plates covered the coffee table and couch.

"Here, come sit down," said Sara, removing debris from a love seat.

Elvin took a seat as Sara suggested as she stood ogling him.

"You're pretty good looking, Elvis," she observed, and then she removed her robe, revealing a black thong and bra.

"Whoa, Sara!" bellowed Elvin, jumping to his feet. "I'm leaving. You're drunk."

"We're all gonna' die so we might as well have some fun while we can, right? The limbs are even falling off the fake cell phone trees," countered Sara, moving toward Elvin.

"Hold on, Sara," said Elvin, extending his arms to block her advance.

What's wrong with a little lovin' before it's all over? It's been so long, and I'm lonely," said Sara, her tone growing desperate.

"I'm sorry," replied Elvin, but I'm married. You know that."

"So go back to your little lady, for chrissakes," snapped Sara, flopping onto the couch causing dirty dishes to fall to the floor.

"Come by tomorrow, okay?" offered Elvin, moving swiftly to the door.

As he departed Sara's house, her crying compounded his own sense of sadness. When he arrived home, he saw that his car was not in the driveway and knew what that meant. Cela had gone to look for her mother. It was several hours later that she reappeared weeping inconsolably. Despite her bad knee, she had made her way to her mother's house and up its stairs to the elder woman's bedroom.

"I saw her. I knew as soon as I opened the door that she was dead. I couldn't bear to look at her face because I could tell a limb had struck it, so I just sat outside in the hall and cried. When I went for help, no one would answer the door. One person threatened to shoot me if I didn't leave his property. I couldn't do anything for Mother. Why didn't you tell me she was dead?"

"There was nothing we could do, honey. I reported it to the police, but they are so overwhelmed, I guess they didn't get to her."

"I can't stand all this. I really can't. My poor mother..." gulped Cela.

"She had a good life, honey. Almost ninety-two. Doubt she felt a thing. Just went in her sleep. When things get cleared up, we'll take care of her. Everything will be okay," reassured Elvin, not believing his own words.

✂

No one appeared the next morning to hear the President's address, and the absence of the usual suspects disturbed the Kells.

"I don't want to listen either. Who does?" declared Cela. "We know that it's over. The news already said everything we need to know. The air is disappearing and we're going to die. End of story."

"They always exaggerate the situation," replied Elvin, searching the radio dial. "It's off the air. The station we usually listen to is not there."

He finally located a distant outlet with a weak signal and heard the voice of the President.

In the Boreas Forest region of Saskatchewan it has been reported that new tree growth has been discovered. A half a dozen Spruce saplings have been found by...

The radio signal faded out and despite Elvin's desperate effort it could not be retrieved.

"Did you hear that, Cela? New trees are growing up north. That could change everything, honey. Restore the oxygen," said Elvin, attempting to cheer his wife.

"But that will take years. Won't it? The news said we don't have much time. Those things take a hundred years to grow," replied Cela.

Although the Kells' food supply was diminishing, Elvin calculated they could last for weeks on what remained. Cela had always kept the cupboards stocked to capacity

"Please eat something, honey," implored Elvin.

His wife had all but stopped eating.

"We have to keep our strength up."

"For what?" answered Cela, leaving her husband alone in the kitchen.

"For one another," replied Elvin.

The radio station signal drifted back for a brief time during which Elvin caught a few more words from the President's latest address.

Every attempt is being made to create oxygen centers, but unfortunately at this time...

"Damn it!" growled Elvin, as the station faded again.

Again he scanned the radio dials for other broadcasts but without success. He wondered if the air was becoming too thin to carry audio waves. For several minutes he stared out of the window down the empty street. It was as still as an early Sunday morning, he thought. Some of his neighbors had obviously abandoned their houses perhaps to be with relatives. Those that remained were clearly keeping to themselves.

Suddenly Elvin caught sight of a figure at the far end of the block moving in his direction. It took a minute for him to realize it was Sara Crosley and that she was naked. As he followed her progress, he noticed she was clutching a large knife. When she reached the front of his house, she stopped.

"Jesus," Elvin mumbled, scrambling to the side door to make sure it was locked.

Sara turned her head toward the house and it was then that Elvin noticed blood on her hands. He was filled with the urge to go to her aid, but the glimmering cutlass in her hand disabused him of that humane notion. Several minutes passed as Sara stood motionless and Elvin peered at her from behind the kitchen window curtain. Her face was expressionless and her eyes appeared unseeing.

"What are you looking at?" inquired his wife, coming up from behind him and causing him to jump.

"Stay still. It's Sara and she's gone nuts. She's naked and has a big knife in her hand."

"What are you talking about?" replied Cela, looking out of the window. "Oh my God. The poor thing. We have to help her."

"She's crazy. Look, she has blood all over her hands. Probably killed somebody," said Elvin, as Cela moved to the door. "Wait. Don't go out there," he shouted, grabbing his wife and holding her in place.

"Let me go! Someone has to help her. Everybody is so heartless now, and you're just like the rest of them," wailed Cela.

"Quiet, she'll hear you. For god's sake, don't get us killed," growled Elvin, continuing to restrain his irate wife.

"Let me go, or I'll never talk to you again," threatened Cela, squirming for freedom.

"Okay, get yourself killed," said Elvin, releasing her.

Cela opened the door and ran outside with Elvin at her heels.

"Where is she?" asked Cela, looking up and down the empty street. "She's gone. Where could she be? Sara!"

"Let's get back in the house," said Elvin, taking Cela by the hand and leading her back to safety.

"She was crazy, honey. Ran off. We're lucky she did. Who knows what she would have done to us."

"She needed help and now who knows what will happen to her?" replied Cela, forlornly.

"We could all use some help," muttered Elvin, locking the door behind them.

❀

Over the next week, Elvin ventured out in his car twice to gauge the situation in his community. The streets were empty except for litter and trash and the markets and hardware stores had all been ransacked. An occasional vehicle would pass and he would search its interior. Desperation invariably filled the expressions of the occupants. As he reached the town's limits, his windshield was pierced with what he assumed was a bullet. He spun his car around and sped down the deserted main street in the direction of home. When he arrived, he found Cela sitting on the front steps.

"Where were you?" she inquired.

"Just driving around. Looking to see if any stores were open. What are you doing out here? It's dangerous."

"I thought maybe Sara would come back."

"Well, it's a good thing she didn't. Let's go inside."

As Cela stood, she lost her footing. Elvin caught her before she hit the ground.

"Are you okay?"

"I've been feeling a little light headed," she replied, holding onto Elvin. "They said that would happen because of the low oxygen. Don't you feel a little dizzy?"

"No, replied Elvin," not admitting that he, too, had experienced bouts of dizziness and some difficulty breathing.

"Did you notice the dead birds? Things are dropping out of the sky," asked Cela, as they slowly moved inside.

"You need to eat something. Lack of nourishment makes you woozy," remarked Elvin, ignoring her comment.

In fact, he had taken notice of many dead animals during his drive around town, and at one point he saw a man collecting animal carcasses. *It's what's for dinner*, he had mused, as he watched the man scamper away with his prized bounty.

"I just want to lay down. I'll eat something later," replied Cela.

Fatigue had become a byproduct of the oxygen depletion, and Elvin also felt the need to rest. When he woke a few hours later, it was dark. Cela continued to sleep as he rose from the bed and went to the kitchen, checking the door locks on his way. He took a seat at the kitchen table and turned on the radio. The only thing he could pick up was an emergency-alert tone emanating from what he assumed was the distant station he had tuned and lost earlier. His breathing was even more forced than it had been before he napped. And suddenly he feared that Cela might have stopped breathing. He dashed to their bedroom and when he arrived he found his wife sitting on the edge of their bed hyperventilating.

"Breath slowly," he urged, putting his arm around her shoulders. "You'll catch your breath if you just relax."

"I want to go," Cela gasped.

"Where, honey? It's late."

"To the forest."

"Forest?"

"Up north. The one with the saplings...the baby trees."

"Why?" asked Elvin.

"I want to see what hope looks like," replied Cela, in a whisper.

For the remainder of the night, the Kells lay arm and arm, and at first light gathered food and bottled water and placed the supplies in the trunk of their car.

"You sure you want to do this?" asked Elvin.

"Yes, I'm sure," replied Cela, whose words were barely discernable.

On their way to the highway that would take them north into Canada, Elvin kept a watchful eye out for the shooter that had fired off a round at him on the outskirts of town. It was a five-mile trek to Route 29, and they made it without incident. When they drove onto the interstate, they saw a couple cars moving in the far distance. Several vehicles stood motionless on the road's shoulders and others sat in different lanes, requiring Elvin to drive around them.

"There's people in the cars. They're all..." uttered Cela.

"Don't look, honey," said Elvin, breathing deeply but finding it nearly impossible to draw in air.

The Kells continued their pilgrimage for several more miles until their car gradually rolled to a stop. Elvin slowly slumped against his wife, whose frozen gaze took in the dying world.

Life and death are one thread,

the same line viewed from different sides.

— **LAO TZU**

THE ADVENT OF AIR

The Wu family had emigrated to the U.S. from the Gansu Province in Northwest China when their only child, Jin, was fourteen years old. Hoping it might help him blend into the new culture they gave him an Anglo first name. But Jason, as he was anointed, had difficulty adjusting to his freshman year in an American high school because he found the English language particularly difficult to master. Despite this, he soon excelled in his schoolwork and ultimately graduated with honors.

In his first year at a prominent New England college, however, Jason was confronted with what seemed an insurmountable challenge. He was required to give a ten-minute talk in his Introduction to American History class. The idea terrified him. The thought of standing in front of his peers drained his lungs, making it nearly impossible for him to utter a word. *They will think I'm stupid because of my bad English*, he thought.

While the prospect of giving a presentation robbed him of sleep, locating a subject he could talk about was not a problem. On several occasions his parents and relatives had spoken about the exploitation of Chinese laborers in the nineteenth century gold fields and construction of the California railroads. At first he found the subject only marginally interesting, but as he searched the topic on the Internet for his class talk, he became keenly engaged by the plight of his forbears. It saddened and angered him to learn how abjectly they had been treated. *I'll let the class know about how terrible America was to these poor men*, he thought with growing purpose. For a moment he felt confident about the assignment, but when he reminded himself that it involved making a speech, his resolve was shaken.

❧

When he focused on his research, his anxiety receded offering him a temporary respite. "The Argon Mining Company and California Central Railroad employed thousands of Chinese workers," stated one website article. He read on.

> During and following their work in the gold mines and on the railroads, Chinese immigrants were persecuted by American workers, who perceived them as competitors for jobs during the major economic downturn in the 1870s. Many Chinese were brutalized and slain and forced removals, known as The Driving Out, resulted in the expulsion from the countryside and cities of a vast number of immigrants, many of them in this country illegally.

A photograph captioned "Miners suffocate in cave!" showing the bodies of several Chinese workers being laid out near the entrance of a mine drew Jason's attention. In another photo, an Asian man of unusual height stood proudly and defiantly before two armed white men. An inscription beneath it stated, "Chinese labor leader Deshi Peng protests mining conditions." In another photo, Peng was shown speaking before a group of his fellow laborers, his arms raised high and his fists clenched. *What a brave man*, thought Jason. His mood suddenly turned dark when yet another photo showed the rights activist being led away in chains. Its caption read, "Troublemaker led to gallows for inciting a riot resulting in two deaths and several injuries."

"That was wrong. So wrong," grumbled Jason. "He was standing up for his people...*my* people."

Jason continued to read the website article and when he finished he was thoroughly committed to informing his class about Deshi Peng's courageous acts. In the two weeks leading up to his class talk, he continued to research the plight of Chinese workers. To his disappointment, however, he did not come across any further information about Peng other than a photo of his newly discovered hero standing on a hangman's scaffolding with several white men clad in black. A rope dangled above Peng's head. There was no account of his actual execution. *They hid this injustice from the public,* he reflected feeling his sorrow and anger increase. He made a copy of the photo and kept it close at hand to help him maintain his indignation over the tragedy.

When the day of Jason's oral presentation arrived, he was filled with feelings of both dread and purpose. He tried his best to concentrate on conveying the important message he wanted to get across in order to dispel his jitters, but he was only partially successful. *Give me strength, Master Peng*, he repeated to himself, as the appointed hour of his great task arrived.

In his seat in the back of the classroom, Jason waited for his name to be called. *I can do this*, he kept repeating to himself while he fought to draw air into his compressed lungs. *This must be how those men felt as the oxygen was used up in that collapsed mine.*

"Mr. Wu, time for your presentation," declared Professor Black.

Jason felt light-headed as he stood before his classmates.

"Go ahead, Jason. Your time starts *now*," said Black, activating his stopwatch.

"My report is on the plight of Chine..." gasped Jason.

It felt as if the last bit of air in his lungs had been used to say those words. He stood staring at his classmates as they returned his stare. Then he noticed the copy of the photograph of Peng had partially slipped from his notebook. He turned to it and was shocked by what he saw. It had morphed into a grotesque scene. The figure he considered his noble ancestor now dangled from the end of the hangman's rope. The sight of it was like an electric charge to him, and he suddenly felt fully restored. His lungs filled with oxygen, and words began to flow forth from his previously frozen lips with a power he had never experience.

"Chinese miners were treated like slaves and forced to work in deadly conditions. They gave their lives so that their American employers could become rich..."

Jason finished his speech with a flourish just as Professor Black announced that his time was up.

As his classmates applauded enthusiastically, his professor nodded in approval. Jason returned to his seat feeling exhilarated and relieved. Yet he was curious about the strange thing that had just happened. *The photo,* he thought, turning to it. *"Dong!"* he blurted in his native tongue.

Again he could not believe his eyes, though this time the transformed picture provided him with great joy. No longer was Deshi Peng dangling from the end of the hangman's rope. He had vanished from the scene, and his executioners stared wild-eyed toward the sky as if their prisoner had floated off into thin air.

It is easy to halve the bread where there is love.

— **IRISH PROVERB**

WHY THE IRISH EAT EARLY

If Colin McKenna didn't make it to his parent's house by five on the dot, chances were very good that his mother would give his dinner away to the Corrigan kids. They were a snot nosed and raggedy lot of neglected brothers who lived a few houses down the lane. His mother had a soft spot for the little urchins, and they knew how and when to exploit that fact. If they didn't see his old Cooper in the driveway by the usual dinner hour, they would show up at the door and perform for handouts—their act consisting mainly of pitiful expressions and stirring entreaties for sustenance.

"Please, Mrs. McKenna, could you give us something to eat? Our mum is sick again, and we have nothing in the pantry. Our stomachs are so empty they grumble like the ghouls."

The compelling pleas of the three neglected Corrigan children, ages seven, nine, and eleven, would invariably touch the heart of Colin's mother.

"Well now, we can't have you going hungry can we? You wait right here, and I'll go and get you something."

That "something" was usually Colin's meal. Not only was it a way for his mother to address the needs of her starving neighbors, but it also served as a dramatic reminder to Colin that dinner was served promptly at five o'clock and not a minute later. Mrs. McKenna was a stickler about this rule and had been his entire life.

"Mum and Da gave us our meal exactly at five each day 'cause one was getting home from work just before then and the other was leaving for work not long after. They wanted the whole family to be at the table while they were both home. It was five o'clock or nothing. No grub if you weren't on time. Go to bed with a hollow belly. My Granny and Granddad ate their evening meal at five, too, and turned in before the dark had come. They climbed from their bed ahead of the morning light to start their chores."

"But that was a different time. You guys aren't farming or working, so why do we have to eat right at five or not at all?" Colin had inquired as a disgruntled adolescent.

"If five was good enough for your ancestors, then it's darn sure good enough for you," his mother had replied.

�֍

Colin had wanted his own place, and the inflexible supper hour was one of the motivating reasons. But living at home was an economical necessity for him after his disastrous marriage came to an end. He was in debt up to his ears and was grateful for the free lodging. Yet he could not wait to be out from under the house rules, which also included lights out at 9 PM (to save on electricity), no overnight guests (not even a male chum), no television shows with violence (comedic or otherwise), all footwear consigned to the entranceway (to spare the carpets from becoming soiled), laundry only on Tuesdays (clothes could not be washed at any other time), baths once a week (another cost saving measure), no snacking or consuming of liquids outside of the kitchen (this one galled Colin as much as the five o'clock supper rule), ad nauseam.

Though Colin was not overly impressed with his mother's cooking, he did have a great passion for one of her dishes—Hunter's Pie. It contained the usual ingredients—carrots, onions, celery, potatoes, and lamb, but the stock had a magnificently unique flavor that defied any attempt to decode its composition. Sweet while a tad spicy, it was better than any he had ever had, and his mother kept the recipe a guarded secret. When he had asked for it, she made it clear she had no plans of ever divulging its contents.

"It's the one hold I know I have on you, sonny boy. You'll always come back to your Mum's for her Hunter's Pie."

"There you have it, laddy," his father had laughed. "Got you by the short hairs for sure."

Although Colin heartily protested, Mrs. McKenna held her ground only agreeing to give him the precious recipe only after she went to her reward.

"I'm making it for supper tonight, so you better be here at five," she declared, and the prospect of his favorite meal brightened his entire day.

❊

As soon as his workday ended, Colin began his commute home. Halfway there an accident caused a major traffic backup, and by the time the road was cleared it was well past five.

"*Cac!*" he shouted in Gaelic."

It was one of only two curse words in the language that he knew, and he used the other next.

"*Feis!*" he bellowed, gunning the accelerator. "There goes my Hunter's Pie, *cac!*"

As he approached home, he saw the three Corrigan brothers moving down the street. The eldest was carrying a brown bag.

My Hunter's Pie! The little blackguards have it! Well, we'll see about that, won't we? he growled to himself, entering his mother's driveway. As soon as he got out of his car, he took off in the direction of the Corrigan boys.

"Hey, stop! Come back here with my dinner!" he yelled at the top of his lungs.

The brothers continued to run toward their house reaching the door just a moment before Colin caught up to them. They ran inside…and he followed. The inside hallway where the boys stood frozen in front of him was dark and smelled of urine and alcohol.

"Mrs. McKenna give us this 'cause we're starving, sir," said the youngster holding the bag.

"Well, it's mine, so give me the bag. Where's your Mum?" asked Colin in a menacing tone.

Before the eldest Corrigan child could respond, Colin ripped the small brown parcel from the boy's hands.

"Mum's sick, sir, and we got no food."

"You mean your old lady is drunk as usual, don't you?"

"No, sir. She's…"

Colin turned and left the house with his meal in hand. His father greeted him as he approached the house.

"Where you going, Da?"

"Thought it be good to get out of the house. Going to the pub for a pint. You might want to come along."

"No thanks, Da," replied Colin, dashing up the steps to his house.

His mother greeted him as soon as he entered.

"What were you doing running down the street like a madman, Colin? And what is that in your hand? It's not the *fuilleach bia* I give the poor Corrigan children, is it?"

"Leftovers?" repeated Colin, opening the satchel.

Sure enough, inside were a few pieces of nearly stale bread and three potatoes.

"I thought…"

"You thought what? That I gave away your cherished Hunter's Pie? Well, I did not, but I should have. You were late again."

"There was an accident. I couldn't help…"

"So then you took the *poundies* and *slim* I gave to those poor little children? That what you done, huh?"

"Sorry, mum."

"You should be! Those Corrigan lads are in harsh times with their drunken mum and dead da."

"Said I was sorry."

"Well, that be so, I suppose I shouldn't waste the Hunter's Pie. Do you still have an appetite for it, son? Suppose you do making such a big fuss of it. Go wash your hands. I'll warm it up. Cold by now."

"Really, mum?

"Go, clean up."

After all that had happened, Colin was delighted that he would still enjoy his favorite dish. When he entered the dining room a few minutes later, his mother was just placing his plate on the table. He quickly sat down, placed his napkin under his chin, and dove into the pie. No sooner had he begun chewing than he spat the food out.

"What did you do to this? It's like a salt lick, for *chrissakes*."

"You deserve nothing better. You know what your Da is always saying, 'Never deny the poor what you have in abundance.' If you can't remember that, then you got no memory at all, Colin? So eat up, me lad. It's your favorite…*isn't* it?"

Mrs. McKenna put on her coat and took a container from the counter.

"Where you going, Mum?" asked Colin, abjectly wiping his tongue with his napkin and grimacing.

"Going to take this *good* piece of Hunter's Pie to them who deserves it."

Colin's mood darkened. *Maybe I'll get that recipe sooner than later,* he thought, as his mother left on her mission of mercy.

" 'I'm very brave generally,' he went on in a low voice."

— LEWIS CARROLL

SOLDIER BOY

Being a soldier had instilled in Carson Tuttle a sense of pride he had lacked. Indeed, in his young mind, soldiering validated his existence. Until he was sworn into the U.S. Army, he was just another high school dropout with few prospects. He wanted his diploma, but his alcoholic father never kept his family in one place long enough for him to receive one. At seventeen, he settled on the military as a way to make something of himself. It took a considerable amount of pleading with his father to sign him into the service, but Carson eventually wore him down. His mother had been in favor of his plan from the beginning, not only because she wanted a better life for him, but also because she was exhausted by the tension that had long existed between her son and husband.

A day after taking the Oath of Allegiance at the induction center in Oakland, California, Carson was in basic training at Fort Ord. Despite his scrawny physique—all one hundred and eighteen pounds of it—and tender years, he excelled at every exercise and capped his eight weeks of training by qualifying as Sharp Shooter on the rifle range. He remained at Fort Ord for clerk school (Basic

Army Administration Course, more popularly known among GIs as "BAAC U") that required another two months of training. The next leg of his military education took him east to Fort Benjamin Harrison in Indiana for a five-week course designed to turn newly minted army clerks into personnel administration specialists, alphanumerically classified by the military hierarchy as grunts with a specialty 716.10 MOS. It was during his time in the Hoosier state that an incident took place, which would follow him throughout his life.

On his first one-day pass, Carson ventured into nearby Indianapolis. He had not found anyone interested in going with him, so he went alone, with no particular goal in mind other than to see what the place looked like. Anything would be a respite from the banality of Army bases, he figured. The drab military buildings did nothing to excite his interest in architecture. He had often dreamed of designing skyscrapers and bridges, but knew that without an education the likelihood of his ever doing so was remote.

A bus stopped just outside the entrance to the base, and it was a quick ride into town. Carson was not overly impressed with the city's structures that looked ordinary and old, artifacts from the nineteenth century. Most large cities in 1964 had modern buildings, but Indy, as everyone seemed to call it, appeared to be the exception. He did find one thing to admire, Monument Circle in the center of the city. He rounded it several times taking in its impressive statuary.

Then he found a small restaurant for lunch. It was empty except for an attractive young woman seated at a table across from the one he chose. When the waitress arrived he ordered a tuna sandwich and a cream soda. After she took his order and left, he noticed the restaurant's only other occupant was looking at him. He nodded and smiled in return.

"You're in the Army. Bet you're at Fort Ben," she said.

"Yes I am," replied Carson, surprised by her words.

"My daddy worked there as a cook 'til his heart attack."

"Is he okay?"

"Nope. He died two years ago. On my own now, since I was fifteen."

"Sorry."

"No, I like being on my own."

"I meant about your father dying."

"Oh, him. He didn't treat us kids good. Always yelling at us after mama passed on. What's your name?"

"Carson."

"That's nice. I never knew a Carson before."

"I was named after my uncle. What's your name?

"Kelly. Kelly Margaret."

"That's a pretty name."

The petite young woman left her table and moved to Carson's.

"Mind if I sit here, Carson?"

"No…that's fine," said Carson standing and offering her a chair.

"You're a polite one. I can see that."

"Thank you."

"I'm not being forward or anything. You seem like a nice guy. I just like to talk to people. My brother says I shouldn't 'cause I could get in trouble talking with strangers."

Carson took in her sweet scent and found her thick auburn hair beautiful. As she spoke, her eyes shimmered like green rhinestones. For the next hour they ran the full gamut of topics within the realm of experiences common to adolescence. The longer they talked the more attractive Kelly became to him.

Still, he wondered if she had some hidden agenda. *Why is she so friendly?* he wondered. He had never encountered a girl so eager to converse with him. *Was she for real? Was he getting into something that would turn out badly?*

When she invited him to walk her home, he agreed though with some reluctance.

"Not too far from here. Maybe seven blocks. Got a small apartment over a shoe repair store. My landlord used to know my dad, so he gives me a break on the rent. Sometimes I think he's flirting with me, but he's pretty old, maybe forty, so I just try to ignore him."

"You have to be careful when you're a girl," observed Carson, becoming more smitten by the young woman by the moment.

"I am," said Kelly, smiling warmly. "You're just the nicest guy. You got any sisters?"

"Two. They're younger than me."

"Bet you watch over them."

"Kind of, but I haven't seen them in a while. Might go home when I finish at Fort Ben. Don't get along with my dad, but he's okay with Kate and Gloria. That's their names. They don't argue with him like I do."

"How about that? We both had daddies we didn't like. I got no sisters. Just a brother like I told you. He watches out for me like a daddy."

Kelly suddenly stopped in front of a shop, causing Carson to bump against her. They both laughed as she announced that they had reached where she lived.

"You want to come up for a little while? It's still early."

Carson accepted her invitation but wondered if he was doing the sensible thing. *Maybe this is where she takes her marks. No, that's ridiculous. Stop thinking that way. She's so sweet and pretty. Really pretty,* he told himself. As he climbed the stairs behind her, he felt a surge of sexual desire more intense than any he had ever experienced. He had never gotten beyond a brief kiss with a member of the opposite sex, and now he felt he might be on the verge of losing his virginity. *Is that what will happen?* he wondered, and then lowered his expectations. *She's probably a virgin, too.*

"Well, here we are. My little penthouse," announced Kelly, unlocking the apartment door. "Come on in."

Kelly turned on an overhead light exposing a shabbily furnished room.

"This is my parlor. Parlor is such a fancy term, don't you think? The kitchenette is over there, and the front room is my bedroom," said Kelly, pointing in one direction and then another. "Let's go sit in my room. It's nice there with the light coming in the big window."

Where is this leading? Carson wondered, feeling both excited and wary.

"Sorry, there's no chairs, so we'll have to sit on my bed."

Carson inspected every corner of the room, expecting someone to leap from the shadows.

"It's a nice room," he said.

"Some of this stuff was my mother's. She had this pink bedspread—its called chenille—and those flowery pillows. I love these things. Reminds me of her."

"Very pretty."

"My daddy never treated her right," commented Kelly, a dark expression replacing her smile.

This prompted further talk about their individual childhoods. The light from outside slowly grew dim, and they found themselves sitting in the twilight. During their conversation they had moved closer to one another, but there had been no physical contact.

"Hey, it's late. You want something to eat?" offered Kelly. "I got some Kraft macaroni and cheese. You like that? I put peas in it. Makes it better."

"No, that's okay, I better go," replied Carson.

"Oh, come on. Eat something. Then you can go back to the base."

Kelly rose from the bed and moved to the door. Carson followed. When they entered the next room, a man about Carson's age rose from the couch and lunged at him, striking him in the mouth.

"What are you doing here?" screamed Kelly, as Carson dashed to the apartment door and threw it open.

"Leave me alone! What are you crazy?" bellowed Carson, running into the hallway and down the stairs.

He could feel blood gush from his upper lip. When he reached the street, he ran as fast as he could away from what he was sure had been a premeditated ambush. *At least they didn't get my wallet*, he told himself, attempting to justify his retreat but feeling craven for doing so. *I should go back and fight. No, there were probably others there. I could have been killed.*

He fished a handkerchief from his pocket as he continued his escape toward the bus stop for his return trip to the base. The cloth was quickly saturated with blood, and he noticed with despair that it had also dripped on his khaki shirt. As best he could, he cleaned himself so people wouldn't notice he'd been attacked. Fortunately, the bus was empty except for Carson and the driver, who didn't even look up from the steering wheel when he climbed aboard. This was not the case, however, when he reached his barracks. Several of his fellow soldiers spotted him when he entered.

"Hey, what the hell happened to you?" asked the guy on the bunk next to his.

"Jesus, you look like you been hit with a baseball bat," observed another fellow soldier across from him.

"Got jumped in town," said Carson, pressing the bloodied cloth to his throbbing wound.

"You kick their ass?"

"No, I figured I was outnumbered."

"How many were there?"

"I couldn't tell. It happened so fast," answered Carson evasively. "They didn't get anything though. I pushed them off and got out of there."

"Where was it?" asked someone. "Let's go down there and beat the crap out of them. Show them if they mess with one of us, they mess with all of us."

The other soldiers agreed and leapt from their beds.

"Thanks, guys. Not worth the trouble you'd get yourselves in. Only got a split lip out of it," responded Carson, hoping to keep the situation from getting out of hand.

Moreover, he did not want his comrades to learn the truth—that he had been attacked by only one guy and had fled like a chicken.

"You probably need stitches. That looks pretty bad," observed one of the soldiers.

"I'll be okay. It stopped bleeding," answered Carson, reclining on his cot.

"Well, I think we should teach those bastards a lesson," grumbled another troop.

"No. That's okay," demurred Carson. "They didn't get what they wanted. That's the main thing. I appreciate it, guys."

It took a while for him to get to sleep, and in the morning, he was shocked by how badly his lip looked. A scab had formed into a dark purple knot that made it difficult for him to speak.

"What happened to you, private?" inquired his division's sergeant.

"I tripped on a curb and hit my face on a fire hydrant."

"Yeah, sure you did," replied his superior skeptically.

A couple days passed and Carson could not get the incident out of his head. *She was so nice,* he kept thinking. *How could she do this?* He began to doubt her complicity in the attack and then to his surprise, he received a telephone call from her.

"Carson, don't hang up. I've been trying to get you. I'm so sorry for what happened. My stupid brother thought we were doing something in my bedroom. When he saw you come out of my bedroom, he really freaked out. When I told him we were only talking he apologized and would like to tell you in person."

"What, so he can jump me again in your apartment?"

"No, really. It was a misunderstanding. Danny is a good brother. He just thinks he's my parent or guardian. If you knew him, you'd like him. Please come over. Nothing bad will happen, I promise. I like you and want to see you again."

"I don't know."

"Please, Carson. My brother is totally embarrassed by what happened. He was going to be a soldier, but he has a heart murmur. Believe me, he won't do anything to hurt you."

"Hurt me? He's lucky I didn't fight back. I'm not scared of him," said Carson indignantly.

"So will you please come over? Danny feels really bad, and I want to see you."

"When?"

"Tomorrow?"

"No, I can't get away during the week. But I could come Friday night after classes."

"Good! Don't change your mind, okay. I want to see you."

During the days that followed, Carson debated the wisdom of returning to Kelly's house, ultimately concluding that it was safe to do so. He mentioned his intentions to his cohorts, and they warned him against doing so, saying it was probably a setup to finish what they had started. Despite their admonitions, on Friday evening he boarded the bus into town. On his walk to Kelly's, he strategized what he would do if her brother made a hostile move on him. The idea of something bad happening dampened his enthusiasm for seeing Kelly. *He might be crazy. Just pretending to be sorry to get another shot at me. Kick him in the nuts as hard as you can, Carson. Then get away and never return...*

Kelly was sitting on the steps of her apartment building when he approached. When she spotted him, she jumped up and ran to him, throwing her arms around him.

"You came! I didn't think you would. Thought you'd back out...I mean, didn't want to see me."

"Your brother here?" inquired Carson, looking up at the apartment's front window.

"He wants to apologize. Don't get mad at him. He doesn't want to fight," said Kelly, resting her head against his arm as they climbed the inside stairway.

"Danny," Kelly called, "we're here."

Her brother emerged from the kitchen with his hand extended.

"Look, man, I'm really sorry. I just thought you were messing with my little sister. She's only fifteen."

Carson looked at Kelly with an expression of surprise mixed with betrayal.

"I thought you were *seventeen*."

"I know. I didn't think you'd be my friend if you knew my real age," muttered the teen contritely.

"You told him you were seventeen, Kelly? Look, I hope you don't hold a grudge over what happened. You can take a sock at me if you want. That lip looks pretty bad."

"No, that's okay," replied Carson, extending his hand to take Danny's.

As they shook hands, three of Carson's Army buddies stormed in and started beating Kelly's shocked brother. Before Carson could fully grasp the situation, Danny was on the floor screaming.

"Leave him alone!!" shouted Kelly coming to her fallen brother's aid.

"Stop it guys! What are you doing here? It was all a mistake. He didn't mean to hit me. He thought I was messing with his baby sister. Leave him alone," pleaded Carson.

After a few more blows, the GIs relented. Kelly kneeled next to her bloodied brother weeping. She then turned her full wrath on Carson.

"How could you do this? I thought you were different. I told you my brother didn't mean to hit you. You had to get your friends to do your fighting? You're a coward! Get out of my house...all of you!" shrieked Kelly, wiping her brother's damaged face with the hem of her skirt. Carson and his fellow troops did as they were told, heading back to the base.

In the years that followed, when asked about the lasting scar, he claimed it was the result of an encounter with the butt of a Viet Cong soldier's rifle. *I did the smart thing. Would have been stupid to fight back. Only make matters worse if I had,* he told himself every time the long-ago incident in Indianapolis entered his mind—which was often. Then he'd be overcome with powerful regret and self-recrimination. *Never run away! Never! Never! You were a soldier. You should have killed the son of a bitch...destroyed him!*

Yes, in the sea of life enisled,
With echoing straits between us thrown,
Dotting the shoreless watery wild,
We mortal millions live alone.

— **MATTHEW ARNOLD**

TRANSED-OCEANIC

Renowned gerontologist and longevity expert Dr. Morley Brittany had spent most of his career searching for a remedy to aging. The focus of his research was a process known as *trans-differentiation*, wherein a *Turritopsis nutricula*—a hydrozoan jellyfish—was capable of regrowing itself endlessly, thus defying extinction. It was on the basis of this singular natural phenomenon that he had theorized that a cell from the species might be injected into another aquatic form to prolong its life. His hypothesis proved to be accurate.

For two years, Morley had introduced *Turritopsis* cells into a vast array of ocean denizens and found that the majority ceased to age. They had been *Transed*, to use the term Dr. Brittany had coined. His work excited his colleagues, who were eager to see what would happen when a jellyfish cytoplasm was given to a primate. They were no more eager than he, since he believed he had discovered the fountain of youth. These were heady days for the research physician, and he was intoxicated by the potential value of his work to benefit humanity as well as his reputation. A Nobel Prize was just one of many things he dreamed might be his.

�֍

As Morley was about to take his experiments to the next level, his world was turned upside down with a diagnosis of Stage IV pancreatic cancer.

"Two to three months, Morley. I'm very sorry. There's really not much we can do other than provide palliative care. I know you realize that."

His longtime friend and prominent oncologist, Larry Cunningham, delivered the devastating news.

"Yes, I'm aware of the prognosis for this, but I can't believe it. I know, denial comes first, but, shit, this can't really be happening to me," replied Morley. "I still feel great…well close to it. No one in my family has ever even *had* cancer, let alone this killer."

"Wish the hell I could do something, but this is one frigging late stage cancer that is nearly impossible to curtail. What do you want to do, Morley?"

"Do I get a choice? If so, I'd like to live. Of all the goddamn times for this to happen to me! I'm right on the verge…Look, I need to get out of here, Larry," said Morley, springing to his feet and all but dashing from Cunningham's office.

Morley sat in his car fighting the urge to drive off the fourth floor landing of the medical building's parking garage. *Get it over quick*, he figured, beginning to hyperventilate. *Why stick around for what's ahead?* A hundred frantic thoughts crowded his mind as he drove home. It was when he turned into his driveway that an idea struck him that instantly lifted his mood. *I could be Transed. Reverse the path of the malignant cells. It could work. What do I have to lose?* Morley put his car in reverse and drove directly to his lab.

❊

Shortly after his staff left for the day, Morley injected himself with a hyper-dose of the sea phylum's T-cells. *Here goes everything.* Over the next week, he continued with the injections with no discernable side effects. However, halfway through the second week of self-administered treatment he noticed a peculiar growth on his lower calf. At first he thought the one-inch excrescence was a thick follicle but on closer examination he discovered it moved. *Cestoidea,* he wondered?

When he removed it, he felt a sharp pain shoot through his leg to his abdomen. *Jesus, it's deep inside.*

"A jellyfish tentacle?" he muttered, staring into a microscope. *How the hell can that be? No, that's impossible. Just couldn't happen...could it?* he pondered.

Morley was relieved when no further growths appeared on his body over the next few days. After a month, the slight abdominal discomfort he had experienced prior to being diagnosed with cancer had disappeared. In fact, he never felt better. *Is it gone? Did it work?* he wondered. *Let's find out.* Morley booked further tests despite his doctor's skepticism.

"Really not necessary, Morley. You were gone over with a fine toothcomb. In fact, I had the results rechecked by Dana Farber, and they confirmed everything we did. I'm glad you're feeling good, but that is often how it goes with this damn thing."

"I want an EUS and some more imaging, Larry. Look I'm not questioning your knowledge. I have the highest regard for you. It's just that something has *happened*..."

"Happened? Jesus, you didn't experiment on yourself with the jellyfish cells…"

"Just run the tests, okay? I'll pay for the damn things myself."

"Fine, but if you're experimenting on yourself, you're violating ethics and protocol. You know that."

"What does someone with late stage pancreatic cancer have to lose, Larry? Stop acting idiotic. C'mon, schedule the tests, for chrissakes!"

"Take it easy. We'll do it at two this afternoon, but you're shooting in the dark, Morley, and you're in for more disappointment. Jellyfish cells are no match for aggressive pancreatic cancer cells."

"Humor me, Larry."

"This isn't a bit funny. If you've been using yourself as a guinea pig, you'll be in deep trouble with the feds and med board.

"And if it worked? What then? Will they take my license away for discovering a remedy for one of the most devastating diseases in existence? I don't think so. See you later, Larry. I have to go visit my miraculous little medusas."

While his staff was at lunch, Morley injected himself with one last blast of T-cells confident in their ability to cure him.

❋

"Amazing!" blurted Larry, reviewing the results of Morley's tests. "This is really extraordinary."

"I knew it worked, but I never thought I'd be the first trial subject. That turns out to be the frosting on the cake. Physician, heal thy self…and I *did!*"

"Now what are you going to do, Morley?"

"On that I need your help."

"How?"

"Patients…*Cancer* patients. I need to verify the results on more patients. Late stagers are the best."

"And you want me to provide you with some, right? Well, what you do to yourself is one thing, Morley, but anything further needs proper approval before it can be tested on actual patients."

"Oh, I'm not an "actual" patient? Shit, Larry. It works. How many more people will die before the FDA gives the go ahead with it?

Little Margie Caufield, thought Dr. Cunningham. *She's so close to the end. This could save her.* "Well, there's this young girl, only twelve, who has very late stage lymphoblastic leukemia, but…"

"But, what, Larry? Let's save her life."

"*But* this is not right, Morley. You know that."

"So you're just going to let her die, even though this could, *no*, this *will* save her?"

"You're playing God, Morley."

"Oh, don't give me that cliché crap, Larry! This is about saving a life when you now have the means to do so."

"Yeah, and when they find out we're doing this, we'll be done…careers over. This violates every rule out there."

"How many terminal patients do you have, Larry?"

"Huh?"

"How many patients in your practice have cancer."

"They all do, I'm an oncologist. That's the kind of patients I have."

"So how many?"

"I don't know, maybe a hundred."

"No wonder you drive a Porsche Carrera GT. I went into the wrong field."

"C'mon, Morley. This is crazy. I'm glad you're in remission, but what you're proposing is patently illegal."

"So you're just going to let all your patients die? Think about it. When we show the medical community and the world that one hundred cancer patients were cured by my method, they'll be astounded and grateful. You think they're going to prosecute us for finding a cure to the most dreaded disease of our time? Jesus, our names will be up there with Salk, Kocher, and Banting. We're going to worry about the rules when we have the chance to change the world for the better?"

"I don't know, Morley..."

"C'mon, let's give your patients back their lives, Larry. How many thousands, millions, of people could be saved by this? This is a remarkable opportunity to do something incredible. It's an obvious decision."

It took more convincing but eventually Dr. Cunningham was on board with Morley's plan. Over the next several weeks, they injected jellyfish T-cells into dozens of patients, who were told they were a part of a very promising new trial that could reverse their cancers.

The initial batch of patient tests taken a month into treatment showed the efficacy of Morley's nostrum. After six months, all of Dr. Cunningham's cancer patients were shown to be free of the disease, although Morley had noticed the same kind of growth he had removed from his calf on two of Cunningham's patients. They had not seemed to take notice, and Morley did not raise the issue fearing Cunningham would want to stop the trial.

"We go public now. I've prepared an overview of our work, and we'll call a news conference, inviting all of your patients to bear testimony," said Morley.

"Maybe we should go slowly. We could get a few noted oncologists to validate our results. It would give us more credibility and mitigate the wrath of the state medical board," replied Cunningham, sounding very tentative.

"Nonsense, we'll make our discovery known to the world in a couple weeks. It will be an auspicious occasion for us, Larry. Stop looking so glum. Do you know what we've done?"

"Yes, I do. Okay, I guess you're right. Two weeks," said Larry, forcing a smile.

✄

They sent out a press release to major news media indicating the time and place for an important news conference that would report "a landmark medical breakthrough." The details were deliberately left vague to arouse curiosity and entice attendance. All of the "Jellies," as Morley came to affectionately call the recipients of the *Turritopsis* cells, agreed to participate in the great event. Thanks to their loyalty to and respect for the two doctors who had seemingly cured them of their dreaded maladies, they were more than happy to cooperate.

Just two days before the scheduled news conference, Morley discovered that he was not alone in another side effect—an insatiable urge to consume small fish and larvae. Nearly all of his patients had contacted him about their similar unusual appetites. Morley assured them that it was just a passing side effect of their treatment, but secretly he wondered if more bizarre changes were ahead for those now carrying substantial amounts of jellyfish T-cells in their bodies.

✄

It fell to Larry Cunningham to gather the media at the designated time for the milestone announcement. But on the morning of the event he was beginning to experience extreme anxiety. It was not because he feared the likely consequences stemming from the news of their unauthorized actions. Despite numerous attempts, he had been unable to contact Morley or any of the other infected cancer patients.

Less than an hour before the scheduled press conference, a television news update regarding a bizarre incident caught Cunningham's attention. He turned up the sound to hear the newscaster say:

There are reports of several people being found paralyzed along the route that leads to Carson Beach. Reporter Steve Evans files this story:

Brian, at least thirteen people were apparently stung by what one spectator described as monster-like creatures with long stringy feelers. Beach resident Kyle Littleton was on his deck overlooking the ocean when he saw something quite extraordinary. Mr. Littleton, please tell us about it.

"Must have been a hundred of these gigantic jellyfish things crawling across the sand toward the water. Never saw anything like it. They just kept coming.

All following this one transparent blob like it was their leader. Then they were gone into the ocean. But if that's not weird enough they made this strange sound...kind of like singing or humming. They seemed *happy*.

If that makes any sense. "

Gertrude has said things tonight it will take
people, including her, ten years to understand.

— **A**LICE **B.** **T**OKLAS

GERTRUDE'S GRAVE

A passage from Ernest Hemingway's memoir, *A Moveable Feast*, never left Otto Niemeyer's thoughts: "If you are lucky enough to have lived in Paris as a young man, then wherever you go for the rest of your life, it stays with you, for Paris is a moveable feast." He had never been to Paris, but he had always hoped to go. His salary as a geography teacher at Jarvis Wile School in Summit, Missouri, had never provided him with the funds necessary to make the trip. Private schools in his part of the world were notoriously cheap to their faculty. It was only after putting aside money from a part time job at an auto parts store following his retirement that he was finally able to realize his long-delayed dream.

Otto planned to visit the haunts of the book's iconic expats. He would patronize the cafes of Montparnasse where Hemingway, Fitzgerald, Joyce and other legendary figures spent long evenings of drinking and jousting with each other. He'd retrace their paths across the City of Light, and he'd visit the graves of Gertrude Stein and Alice B. Toklas in the Père Lachaise Cemetery. Of all the characters in Hemingway's reminiscence, Stein and Toklas held a special fascination for him. It was their devotion to one another that most caught his fancy. That the two women had found each other in a world hostile to unconventional couplings had given him hope. Although he was straight, their relationship served as a beacon in the lonely sea of his existence. A lifelong bachelor, Otto had spent his entire adulthood without a significant other.

While he was not a big fan of Stein's prose style—*What the hell did* "There ain't no answer. There ain't gonna be any answer. There never has been an answer. That's the answer." or "There is no there there" *mean?* He did enjoy her apparent playfulness with words but was nonplussed by their ambiguity or perhaps it was his lack of comprehending their intended meaning. Still, he admired her deeply and truly looked forward to paying homage to her and the woman who had been her closest consort. The idea that he would be in such close proximity to their remains thrilled him and gave him a sense that he might somehow become a part of their fabled oeuvre.

While his knowledge of the French language was modest, he felt confident it would not pose a problem, and his arthritic knees were still capable of withstanding hearty walks. It was in this heightened frame of mind that Otto boarded a plane to New York that would connect with a flight to France. He could not have been happier, and he uncharacteristically engaged with as many fellow travelers as he could to share his joy. It was one of the brightest times in his life—a life that had been awash in monotones of grey. Even his childhood, with older parents, had been a lackluster and unmemorable affair. Like Otto, his mother and father had also taught at Jarvis Wile School their entire careers, and like him, they, too, had been forced to stay close to home because of a lack of resources to do otherwise.

The day after arriving in Paris, Otto took a cab to the Père Lachaise Cemetery. He had first planned to visit the Eiffel Tower and the Louvre, but his powerful urge to visit the resting place of his literary heroines prompted him to revise his plan. After being deposited at the tree-enshrouded entrance of the graveyard, Otto began to stroll down the main path. He was surprised to see the gravestones crammed so closely. He had never seen such a crowded burial ground and was glad he had purchased a map of the site in advance of his visit. It would have been impossible to achieve his purpose otherwise, he concluded. The map included information about the graveyard that amazed Otto. More than seventy thousand resided in this city of the dead spread over more than one hundred acres. The five thousand trees lining the gravel lanes delighted him, and the shadows they cast were stenciled to the ground by a vibrant June sun. The effect was captivating and almost otherworldly to Otto, and he could not conceive of a lovelier place to spend the hereafter.

I'm coming, dear Gertrude, he thought excitedly, as he checked the directory on the back of the map labeled "Noted Occupants." He quickly ran his finger down the long alphabetized column. *There she is.* He could hardly contain his excitement when he came to her name. I'm coming, *Le Stein*, said Otto, using the sobriquet given to her by her celebrated coterie. When he reached the grande dame's grave, he was surprised and somewhat disappointed by how unadorned it appeared set next to a small, yellow storage building. *Oh, Meme Moderne, you deserve better*, he mumbled to himself, as he knelt close to her headstone. "How you must long for your beloved *rue de Fleurus*," he whispered sympathetically.

As Otto backed away from the decrepit monument, he was certain he heard a female voice intone, "A grave is grave unless it is not grave." *Yes,* he thought, *yes, of course, dear Gertrude. How could one be grave among friends and lovers? Now those words I understand. Merci, Le Stein.*

Referring to the plot directory again to find the Toklas site, he suddenly became aware that they were just two of a myriad of renowned fellow tenants. He had been so focused on locating Stein that he had failed to see who else was interred in the sacred ground around her. His eyes widened in amazement as they ran down the list: Apollinaire, Balzac, Bernhardt, Bizet, Calas, Chopin, Debussy, Delacroix, Ernst, Pissarro, Seurat…Otto was overcome with the realization that he stood among the remains of some of the world's most renowned cultural figures. He immediately became obsessed with the idea of becoming an occupant of the hallowed necropolis upon his passing. *It would be so wonderful to spend eternity with such extraordinary people. I must…I must.*

✄

Over the next several days, Otto paid his respects to many of the other famous occupants of Père Lachaise. He had also contacted its office to inquire about the possibility of being buried there. The cost of purchasing a plot was formidable, however, and was laden with conditions. An individual had to die in Paris in order to be eligible and sign a renewable lease of ten, thirty, or fifty years— the longer the lease, the more expensive. Since plots were limited, if a lease expired, the remains would be removed and relocated. A body could be cremated and placed in the cemetery's columbarium for less expense, but that did not appeal to Otto. His deepest wish was to share the cemetery's soil with its deceased luminaries. He believed that to rest among them would add meaning and weight to his otherwise jejune existence.

Otto figured that in order to purchase the plot he would have to do something drastic to raise the money, and he knew what that meant. He would have to sell his mother's engagement ring, which he had inherited long ago. The formidable diamond had been handed down through generations of Niemeyers and was worth a considerable sum. While it disturbed him to depart with it, he justified doing so since there had never been anyone to give it to. He had not married and the prospects of getting engaged at his age were less than remote.

He put a down payment on the plot with a credit card, agreeing to pay the balance within thirty days, and returned to the States feeling positively exuberant. While Otto had little to look forward to in what remained of his daily life, he now believed that in death he would achieve fulfillment. Spending eternity with the great and glorious was far better than living in his mundane world.

❦

Otto located a buyer for his mother's ring, and to his satisfaction the sum it brought was in excess of the money he needed to pay off his gravesite. He put the balance in the bank in anticipation of an eventual return trip to Paris when he felt his demise was nearing. Fearing that he might suffer a fatal accident before his time came, he substantially decreased his already nominal presence in the outside world by remaining in his small house as much as possible.

Thus the years passed slowly and without notable incident until he suffered a minor heart attack. That prompted him to execute his long-planned end-of-days strategy.

"You need a repair of your left ventricle. It's a delicate operation, but you should come out of it okay, Mr. Niemeyer," said a coronary specialist at Summit Hospital, where he had been taken.

Upon hearing the doctor's words, the seventy-six year old patient decided to sell off everything he owned and cash in his retirement investments for his return to Paris. Immediately after his release from the hospital, Otto set about to clear the path back to the Père Lachaise Cemetery for his rendezvous with Stein and her distinguished neighbors.

Je reviendrai bientot, Le Stein, thought Otto, and *soon* it was. Within two months Otto had rented a small room near the cemetery in the 20th Arrondissement. While it cost considerably more than his previous dwelling in the poorer 19th Arrondissement, Otto felt that since his days were numbered his finances would more than suffice for the time that remained. He was surprised and a bit chagrinned when months passed and his health did not deteriorate as he had expected it would.

Indeed, the better part of a year passed while Otto impatiently waited for his end to come. During that time he had visited Père Lachaise nearly every day and had long conversations with many of the cemetery's notables. Of course, among the most loquacious was Gertrude herself, who regaled him with countless anecdotes and tales of the Lost Generation. Otto could not wait to enter the afterlife with such intriguing and engaging friends. But his wait felt endless until the day before his birthday.

On his brief walk to the cemetery up a narrow street, Otto encountered two youths who looked intimidating.

"You American, huh?"

Otto attempted to ignore them and continue on his way, but his path was blocked.

"Give us your things now! *Je te tuerai!*" threatened the smaller of the two.

When Otto hesitated, the second youth pulled out a knife.

"*Actuellement!*" he growled.

Otto handed over his wallet, watch, and signet ring, and expected the youths to leave him alone.

"Your *jaquette*. What is there?"

"Nothing. Just some papers of no value," answered Otto, hoping they would not take the cemetery lease that he always carried with him in the event of his imminent heart attack.

"Give them to us!" demanded his assailants rifling through his pockets and removing the papers.

"Please, they are worthless," pleaded Otto.

"*Non, un vieux homme!*" replied the teenager clutching the cemetery lease.

Both young men then turned and ran with Otto in slow pursuit.

"Keep everything, but give me back those papers!" shouted Otto in the direction of their vanishing figures.

As he lumbered across the street he became dizzy and fell, striking his head against the curb with great force. And it was there that he died.

When the police examined his body the only identification they found was an address on the elderly man's medical alert bracelet. After French officials contacted authorities in the States, Otto's remains were returned to Summit, Missouri. There he was buried with little fanfare in one of the town's two cemeteries. A modest headstone engraved with just his first name was placed next to Estelle and Harold Niemeyer's graves. Otto's parents had purchased the plot for their only child when he was born.

False manners feed on deceit.

— **TOBRA CORNICK**

POLITE CAKE

"You take the last piece," implored Katy.

"No, no! I'm full...*really*," replied Libby, holding her hands up in feigned protest. "You eat it, Kenny, honey."

"Thought you didn't want a chubby hubby," replied her spouse, his eyes fixed on the dispossessed nugget of Black Forest layer cake.

"Guess it falls to you, Ben," declared Katy, gesturing toward the table.

"No room left in this bear's belly. Sorry. I'm out of the running," claimed Ben, his gaze resting on the vestige of what had been the shared dessert.

For a minute the two couples silently surveyed the surviving morsel and one another. Then the Johnsons and Harrisons resumed what was becoming a tense exchange.

"Well, *someone* should eat it," pressed Libby, peering at the fudgy leftover.

"Go for it, honey," urged her husband, measuring her intent.

"Yeah, it's a shame to let it go to waste," added Ben, calculatingly.

"Oh, for God's sake! *I'll* eat it!" blurted Katy.

Her dinner companions sat frozen in disbelief as she lifted the sugary remnant to her mouth and gulped it down. Several moments of stunned silence ensued and then her tablemates stood up and stomped away angrily.

The last words Katy heard from her retreating compeers were *selfish bitch*! Wiping frosting from her lips as she sat alone in the restaurant, Katy felt pleased that she had taken the remaining bite of the cake.

The hope I dreamed of was a dream,
Was but a dream, and now I wake.
— **CHRISTINA ROSSETTI**

SEEING GEORGE

We had pulled up to the curb on Thayer Street on the East Side of Providence, a few blocks up from the Avon Theater. It was where we usually found a place to park on the busy thoroughfare. As I turned off the engine, I looked down the street about a half a block and noticed a man approaching in a flowing overcoat carrying shopping bags. There was a dull ring of recognition, a mild sense of familiarity about the person. Maybe I knew the guy, I thought. My wife was gathering her scarf and gloves to face the cold December air as I continued to peer at the nearing figure. And then *BAM!* It hit me.

"Oh my God, it's George Harrison!" I blurted!

"What?" my wife replied.

"George Harrison!" I repeated with urgency.

"Where? *C'mon…*"

"Coming up the street. *Look!*" I pointed.

She moved closer to the windshield for a better view.

"It can't…He does kind of look…You think?" she gasped.

We both sat frozen in disbelief as the former Beatle was now within a few feet of our car.

"How could it be, Jacob? What would he be doing here?" sputtered Emily.

"I don't know, but it's him," I insisted, having no doubt at all.

As the legendary performer passed, he gave us a quick sideways glance, which I returned with a broad smile of recognition. Emily jumped from the car and pursued him, as I tried to dissuade her. She ignored my plea as I watched Harrison move away through the rearview mirror.

✄

"George! George!" Emily shouted as he rounded the corner.

"Hon, leave the poor man alone," I said, as we caught up to him. "She's...I mean, *we* are huge admirers of yours, George," I said apologetically.

"Love you, George!" exclaimed Emily as the ageless rocker continued on his way.

"Me, too, George," I added.

To our amazement the fabled singer suddenly stopped and turned around.

"Thank you, folks. I appreciate that," he said softly.

"Why are you here? I mean in Providence of all places," inquired Emily, moving closer to Harrison.

"Visiting my son for the holidays. He attends Brown."

Is this actually happening? Are we really having a conversation with one of the Fab Four? A hundred questions filled my head. *Do you miss John? What's your relationship with the other two Beatles? Did Yoko really breakup the group...?*

"My husband teaches at URI...the University of Rhode Island," replied Emily, star struck but still able to find the words to keep the dialogue going, which was more than I could do.

"Good school, I hear," replied George.

"I'm Emily and this is my husband, Jacob."

George extended his hand and we excitedly shook it.

"Are you here for long?" asked Emily.

"Just a couple of more days."

"It must be hard moving about with people like us stopping you."

"Surprisingly not. The students don't recognize us old crooners like they used to."

"Yeah, it's us oldies that recognize you goodies," said Emily, and I thought, *Well, that will kill it.*

Instead of being put off by her awkward attempt at levity, Harrison laughed.

"Say, would you folks care for some hot tea? It's bone chilly out here, and the house that I'm staying in is just around the corner."

"You mean with you?" I was able to ask despite my shock at the invitation.

"Really, George?" chirped my wife in sheer delight.

"I'm not seeing my son again until the morning, so I could use a little company. What do you say?"

"Oh, my God, yes!!" answered Emily, about to burst with joy.

"Are you sure?" I asked, praying he was.

"No, not really," said George, with an impish grin. "Of course, I'm sure. Follow me."

This can't be happening. Tea with a Beatle, I thought, and I could tell that Emily was thinking the same thing. We followed Harrison in silence expecting to wake up from our fantasy at any moment.

"You live around here?" asked Harrison

"Off Hope. We live off Hope...*Street*. Just up the way."

George chuckled. "Guess we all live off Hope, don't we? Well, here we are. This old manse belongs to the university and is loaned out to certain visitors. They keep a housekeeper and cook here. Otherwise it's a hulking emptiness. Come on in."

"Lovely," said Emily, as we climbed the steps leading to the entrance of the brownstone Victorian.

"Meets the needs," replied Harrison impassively

The interior of the house struck us as the epitome of old world elegance.

"Let's sit in the drawing room. We can take our tea there. Care for something to eat? I can have the cook whip something up."

"Oh, please, don't inconvenience anybody. Tea is just fine."

"Well, it's no inconvenience. That's her job."

"Really, George, you're too kind. We were going to grab something at Andrea's before the movie."

"Oh, dear. I've disrupted your plans. You'll miss the film."

"Being here with you is far better than any film," said Emily adoringly, and I concurred.

"This is an exceptional treat for us, George. No one will *ever* believe this."

"Well, it's nice to have a little company. I really had nothing planned for the evening, so you're kind to spend a little time with me."

"Our pleasure a hundredfold, George," responded Emily.

Again I concurred with my wife and ventured a question, hoping not to upset him with what he might consider as his personal business. "Your wife didn't join you on this visit to the States?"

"Actually she did, but she left for New York to attend a gallery opening of a friend. She'll be back tomorrow and then we'll be off to home the next day."

At that moment, the caretaker entered the room and asked George if he would like anything. Turning to us, he asked whether we'd prefer coffee to tea. Although neither of us were really tea drinkers, we both replied that we'd love a hot cup of tea. It seemed the correct thing to do around a Brit. Moreover, we did not want to seem demanding.

"Three teas then, Mrs...."

"Murphy, sir," replied the middle-aged women.

"Yes, sorry. I'm not great with names. Could we have some dunkers, too?"

"Yes, sir."

The woman left the room, and George pointed to a leather couch and told us to make ourselves comfortable. Still in something of a daze, we heeded his directions. A guitar leaned against the arm of the wingback chair he sat in.

"Are you working on a new song, George?" I braved.

"Actually, I've been fiddling with a little tune since last night. At this point, it's really just a germ of an idea."

Harrison lifted the guitar, and ran his fingers across the strings. He then began to sing along with his new composition. Chills ran up my spine. About a minute into it he stopped.

"That's as far as it's gotten to this point. Haven't found a hook yet, and I'm not crazy about the words."

"Would you play it again, please?" asked Emily.

Harrison nodded and replayed the song fragment.

"Stymied where to take it from here, but it will come. Always does."

"Do you mind if I make a suggestion?" said Emily, timidly.

"You a musician?"

"I play a little piano. Have since I been small. But, I'm not a professional. I do hear things though...melodies."

"Great! Tell me what you hear, Emily," said George with an encouraging smile.

"Would you play it one more time?"

"Sure."

When he stopped, Emily hummed her idea.

"Could you repeat it?" requested Harrison.

In a fuller voice, Emily performed her theme line.

"Hey, that's nice. Let me try it," said George.

When he was through, he beamed with satisfaction. "Damn that's a hell of a hook! Can I use it?"

"Really?" Emily squealed. "Of course. I'd be so honored. I can't believe it. Oh, my God. I'm writing a song with a Beatle."

"*Former* Beatle, "said George, amused by Emily's nearly manic enthusiasm.

During all this a lyric had come to me that I thought might improve upon Harrison's, but it was only my wife's show of bravado made me dare to say so.

"Please don't take this the wrong way, George, but I have a piece of lyric that might work. I used to write words to songs when I was younger, though I can't read a note of music. Would you care to hear it?"

I held my breath as one of the world's great pop song writers replied. "Well, why not, Jacob. May as well make this a community effort."

"If instead of the line 'Talking to the moving clouds,' you sang 'Riding on the tropic breeze,' it might fit better...probably not. I'm way out of my depths and a fool for suggesting different lyrics to a George Harrison song. Man, that's brazen. Sorry."

"Let me try it with Emily's hook."

After playing the partially written tune twice with the suggested revisions, Harrison put the guitar down, stood up, extended his arms, and requested a group hug.

"You guys have done it. This is going to be great. I love it. It's all but finished with your help, and I'm going to list you as co-writers. My sweet lord, you've made us a hit. Let's write another song together—maybe even a whole album. How about…?"

From far off, I could hear Emily calling me. Then a brilliant shard of light from the setting sun pierced the windshield and temporarily blinded me.

"Jacob! Jacob! George turned back and smiled at me when he was almost at the end of the block. Do you believe that? Jacob? Hello? What's the matter with you?"

"Oh, nothing." I mumbled, feeling the full weight of reality descend on me. "I was just daydreaming."

Jump up as far as you can. See how far you get.

— **JOSEPH PAUL**

THE RULES OF GRAVITY

When his divorce proceedings began, Sid Barrington had been advised by his attorney to avoid dating for at least a year to get his head back in a healthy place. He did as his lawyer suggested, but one year turned into two and then three. It wasn't that he was deliberately avoiding the dating scene. He just couldn't find anyone he wanted to go out with. Not that he tried very hard to make it happen. Then things changed when a young woman joined his company. She caught his eye instantly, and for weeks he watched as she settled into her job as the billing clerk for the flooring outlet where he worked as a buyer. He gradually developed a casual friendship with the woman and finally gathered the courage to ask her out. She accepted and he was happier than he had been since the collapse of his marriage.

Sarah Pendleton. I even love the sound of her name, he thought excitedly, as he readied himself for his date. *God, I hope it goes well.* His nerves were raw at the prospect of his first hookup with the woman who had grown more attractive to him with each passing day. *Don't blow it, Sid. Don't blow it. Oh, shit, I probably will. Look, my palms are sweaty. Maybe a drink?* Sid rarely consumed alcohol, but on this occasion he figured it might settle him down some. He poured himself a substantial shot of Wild Turkey, a gift given him by his brother a dozen years earlier, and downed it in one gulp. For a few moments he thought he would suffocate because he was unable to catch his breath as the liquor coursed through his system. When he finally was able to inhale, he nearly vomited. *Oh, God, that's awful stuff!*

It took Sid a few more moments to get past the jarring experience, and when he had he could feel the effects of the powerful beverage. *Whoa! That's strong booze!* he reflected, heading out of his condo. As he drove from his driveway, he struck the garbage can awaiting pickup by the curb. *Easy, buddy. Don't get a DUI.* Halfway down his block, he felt something hit his bumper. *What the...!* Peering through his rear view mirror, all he could see was the blackness of night. *Another garbage can*, he thought, continuing on his way.

The remainder of his drive to meet Sarah at the cinema went without incident. By the time he arrived he figured most of the whiskey's effect was gone, but it had done its job by relaxing him. When he caught a glimpse of Sarah standing near the ticket window, all he felt was excitement. *God, she's pretty!* Unfortunately, over the course of the evening he discovered that she was more physically attractive than intellectually interesting. Throughout their dinner following the movie, she mostly talked about her two Siamese cats. When Sid tried to redirect the conversation, she would steer it back to her beloved felines.

"Would you like to meet Mimi and Pierre?" asked Sarah. "You can come to my place for coffee, if you want."

Sid demurred, saying he had an early rise to drive up to his brother's in Hartford, a few hours drive north of Baltimore. This was a pure fabrication, because by the end of the evening, he had lost interest in pursuing the striking brunette. While appearance was important to Sid, the substance of an individual's personality was of equal or even greater consequence to him. In that area, he found her a totally lacking. He was surprised and disappointed, because she had seemed so much more engaging at work.

Although they never went out again, they continued to be cordial to one another in the workplace. Two years after their only date, Sarah would leave the floor-covering company to be married.

✂

The next morning a TV report caught Sid's attention. His neighbor had been the victim of a hit and run right on his street. It took him only a second to connect the dots. *Was that what I hit last night? Oh, my God!!* The person he now was convinced he had struck was well known to him, because he had been regarded as the scourge of the neighborhood since he and his wife arrived from Australia two years ago. Trevor Collins was a brute, and his wife was a lout as well. Both had alienated the residents of Furlong Drive with their callous behavior and blatant disregard for the appearance of their raised ranch and its surroundings. When neighbors had petitioned the couple to rid their yard of an assortment of debris—mostly rusting and decaying objects and plastic containers and soda bottles—they had been greeted with threats.

At least he's not dead, thought Sid, his panic rising. *And no one apparently saw me hit him.* Upon inspecting his car's bumper, he was relieved to find it undamaged. *Maybe it wasn't me.* But on closer inspection, a piece of red flannel hanging from beneath the fender convinced him otherwise. *His shirt...he was wearing a red flannel shirt the last time I saw him. Shit! What am I going to do? Go to the police? I'll go to jail! Hell, no! That can't happen. Nobody saw the driver. What about Trevor? The news says he has a concussion and broken bones but no recollection of the incident. Don't do anything.*

And so it was that Sid tried to put the mishap behind him, though he was not successful. His guilt weighed on him and forced him to confront his victim. A week after Trevor returned home from the hospital, Sid decided to pay him what he hoped would be a friendly visit. He had to know if Trevor had any inkling that he was the one who ran him down. If he did, he would try to make amends. Just how he wasn't sure. Since neither Trevor nor his wife had made an attempt to contact him, he felt he was likely in the clear, but he had to be certain.

"Yeah, what you need?" mumbled Sybil Collins, answering his knock—the doorbell was apparently not working.

"Hello, Mrs. Collins. I'm Sid. I just thought I'd check to see how your husband is doing," replied Sid, tentatively.

"Really? Trevor, you got company!"

The disheveled-looking woman waved for Sid to enter. The inside of the house was in no better shape than the outside. The furniture looked as if had been purchased at a flea market and old newspapers and magazines were stacked everywhere.

"Who is it?" called Trevor from another room.

"It's Sam from down the street."

"Sid…It's *Sid*."

"Get your butt out here, hon!"

Trevor entered the room on crutches. A soiled bandage covered a section of his head, which had been partially shaved.

"Yeah, what can I do for you, mate? I'm in a bit of pain here."

"Just want to see if you need anything?"

"We need *something* all right," blurted Mrs. Collins. "We need to find the bugger who done this to him."

"They don't know who did it?" inquired Sid.

"Naw, they'll never find the ratbag who hit him."

"You never know, Sibby. These jackals usually are found out," said Trevor, flopping into a chair. "Can you get me and...what's your tag?"

"Sid."

"Yeah, Sid, a beer. Would you like one?" asked Trevor, pointing to Sid with his cane.

"I'm fine. Not much on the booze."

"One of them tight-ass tea teetotalers eh? Well, just don't stand there, Sibby, get me a Fosters."

"Hold your horses," replied Sybil, trailing off to the kitchen.

"Some chips, too, while you're at it."

As soon as she was out of the room, Trevor began to snicker while staring at Sid.

"Guess we both know, don't we?" asked Trevor, arching his eyebrow.

"Know what?" replied Sid, baffled.

"That you were the one runned over me."

"Me?"

"Yeah, you. Got a look at your car before going under. A Jeep Cherokee, right?"

Sid was at a total loss for words. He felt like his heart would pound its way through his chest.

"That's what I thought. Guess I should call the cops. Unless we can work this out between us."

"I didn't mean to...It was an accident."

"Nearly killed me. Bad blow to the head and my ankle is all broken up. That should be worth some major compensation. Wouldn't you think...*mate*?"

"What do you have in mind?" asked Sid, feeling his world collapse around him.

"A monthly payment would help ease the pain. I may not be able to walk right again. How am I supposed to work construction if I'm disabled?"

"How much?"

"Let's say five hundred dollars a month for life. That seems reasonable considering. Don't it, Sid? I mean I could sue your Yank ass for a hell of a lot more."

"That's a lot. Okay…fine."

"And don't say nothing to the missus," said Trevor, his forefinger over his lips as his wife reentered the room. "Where you been? Thought I'd never see you again."

"Oh, shut your yap, you old bludger. Here's your bloody beer and chips."

"Well, I guess I'll be going now, Mrs. Collins," said Sid, turning to leave.

"Keep in touch," responded Trevor, with a complicit wink.

"I will. Definitely. Thank you."

On his return home, Sid reached the conclusion that it might have been better for him if he had killed Trevor rather than merely maiming him.

❄

Two days later, Sid received a phone call from Trevor advising him how to get him the agreed upon monthly payment.

"Cash only. No checks. Just put it under the front door mat on the first of each month. Best to do it after it gets dark so the missus don't see you. Got that, mate?"

As the years went by, the monthly compensation Sid was obliged to provide Trevor increased twofold. Eventually it became a financial burden to him, especially after the business he had been employed by for nearly twenties years went bankrupt and had to lay off its entire staff. Sid had managed to save a decent sum, since he had few expenses, but he could foresee a time when he might not be able to payoff his hit and run victim. *What the hell would happen then?* Sid wondered. *He's been extorting me for five years. If he says anything, he'll be in deep trouble, too*, he reasoned. *I should just stop paying the prick. Call his bluff.*

But Sid did not have to confront his blackmailer because he had fallen to his death from the scaffolding of a high-rise under construction. *That's it. I'm out from under. No more monthly payments*, thought Sid, dialing the number of the funeral home where Trevor Collins was to be waked. At seven that evening he would bid his worst nightmare adieu and take back his life. For the first time in months, Sid felt optimistic about his future prospects. An interview the previous week had resulted in a callback for a second one, and Sid felt confident that he would soon end his period of economic strife, if not the continuing drought that made up his so-called love life.

✂

It did not surprise Sid that the parking lot of the funeral home was mostly empty. There was no more than a half dozen attendees inside and none appeared to be in a state of mourning. As Sid approached Mrs. Collins, he caught part of her conversation.

"It was that crushed ankle of his from that hit and run. Couldn't keep weight on it for very long. Probably why he fell. Never too sure-footed after being run over."

The couple she had been addressing nodded and moved away leaving the new widow alone.

"Hello, Mrs. Collins. I'm very sorry for your loss," said Sid, extending his hand.

"Thank you. You're Sam from down the street."

"Sid, *Sid* Barrington, from number seventy-two."

"Oh yeah, you came to our house after Trevor's accident. I remember."

"Did he ever find out who ran over him?" inquired Sid, wiping his moist palms against his pants

"Oh yeah, he knew who hit him."

Sid gulped sensing he was nearing the edge of a cliff. "He did?"

"It was his stupid cousin, Quinn. Confessed not long after you visited us, as a matter of fact. Trevor wouldn't tell the cops. Kept it a secret. Didn't want his kin to get into trouble. Don't know why. His cousin sure wasn't any treasure. Now it don't matter anymore, does it?"

"No…No, I guess it doesn't," answered Sid, catching his deflated image in the polished side of Trevor's coffin.

Strangers' gifts are no gifts and do no good.

— **SOPHOCLES**

DISTANT GESTURE

Life forms from the Dracon Galaxy wanted direct contact with Earthlings. They had successfully connected with the occupants of many other planets in many different galaxies. But Earth was the only one that had so negatively depicted aliens in its entertainment media that it posed a genuine danger to visit. Dracons concluded that any foreign species landing on the planet would likely be greeted with hostility, unless the citizens of the small blue world were convinced they were under no threat. Since Dracons appeared spider-like, they knew it would be a tough sell. It struck them as a strange coincidence that Earthlings were especially appalled at the form of any creature with multiple tentacles. *Why would that not seem an obvious advantage over having only two limbs?* they speculated.

The first thing that occurred to the aliens was to change their appearance to keep from frightening the Earthlings, but then they realized, too, that any visitors coming from outside of their world—regardless of their appearance—would be immediately suspected of evil intentions. Therefore, members of the Dracon High Council agreed that it must first create a receptive atmosphere before a visit to Earth was made. The next question was how to accomplish this.

"They are a warring tribe, so we must make them believe we are benevolent, and then they will befriend us," offered Saglon Purt, the council's Deputy Chief.

"Yes, but how do we do that?" asked Lord Cupleta from his ornate rostrum.

"They are plagued with countless infirmities. Many are deadly to them. If we cure them of these diseases, they will surely welcome us. Even the worst things they suffer are of a low-grade, highly curable nature," observed Ambassador of Interventions, Litor Klim.

"Is that not our standard procedure upon encountering a new species?" inquired Purt.

"Yes, we sanitize the creatures of every world we enter, so this will require no new procedures, other than making the Earthlings aware that we will vanquish their ills. They will see it as a great gift and we will be able to gain their admiration and trust, which is what we seek in order to benefit from what they possess," replied Klim.

"So be it. Prepare to make contact with the Earthlings. Send a series of messages, indicating our wish to befriend them. Explain that we mean them well and shall prove it by eliminating all afflictions from their planet. Then activate the Panacea Wave. When they realize we have done so, we will commence our visit with their blessing."

✄

The first message from Draco reached SETI and NASA on June 10, 2038. Initially, staff at both centers was skeptical about the communication they received because it came in the form of a Picasso's dove lithograph with the famous 1960s peace symbol floating above it.

The words, "We wish you love and peace from Draco," were inscribed in lavish script at the base of the image that filled all the computer screens at the two facilities.

"We been hacked again," shouted Casey Dwight, Senior Research Scientist at SETI. "Track the origin."

"It's not coming from here," replied Instrument Specialist Perry Brown. "I mean it's not coming from this planet."

"Huh?" responded Casey, moving to Perry's workstation.

"My coordinates have it originating in the central part of the Draco Dwarf constellation. Here it is. Right ascension 17h 20 m 12.4s and declination +57 54' 55". Apparent magnitude 10.9."

"Check the system. See if it's experiencing any anomalies," directed Casey.

"Nope. Everything reads out okay," reported Perry, after a quick examination of several small screens.

"Incoming stream from NASA," noted SETI Communication Specialist, Sarah Belrose.

"All right," replied Casey. "Bring it up."

"Dr. Dwight, are you getting what we're getting?" asked Bill Wiley, NASA Chief of Operations.

"If you're talking about art work from another galaxy, the answer is yes."

"What do you make of it? Can you verify it? Shit, if so, we're about to witness the greatest event in human history."

"All of our checks from here confirm its origin, but beyond that, who knows? Maybe it's some kind of a super beam from Earth that's bouncing back from the Draco Dwarf region," speculated Casey.

"That would be one hell of a beam," commented Wiley, sounding mystified. "We're investigating it here, and so far we confirm your findings. Hold on. Do you guys hear that?"

"Music?" responded Casey.

"It sounds like...*like*, 'What the World Needs Now is Love,'" said Wiley.

"Bacharach," mumbled Casey.

"What?" asked Wiley.

"It's a Burt Bacharach song. My dad loved it."

"Your father an alien?" asked Wiley, jokingly.

As the music played, a message began to fill the monitors at both NASA and SETI.

We are your friends from the Draco Dwarf Galaxy. We wish to visit your planet but realize your people fear outsiders...those from other worlds. We are peace-loving life forms with technology far more advanced than yours. It is our mission to make contact with other species throughout the universe to learn and benefit from their unique existences.

To prove we wish all humans well, we will eradicate all illnesses and diseases from Earth. Once there is no longer any pestilence or harmful bacteria attacking your bodies, we will ask your permission to visit. We do not look like you, and our appearance may at first disturb you. But we hope our actions will prove to you that we are no different than you. We will now send you a live transmission to show you what we look like.

Please do not panic.

The SETI and NASA monitors became a hash of pixels that slowly amalgamated to reveal the extraterrestrials.

"Jesus!" blurted Perry, at what appeared to be a nest of giant insects.

We look at you as you look at us, but as your appearance becomes less foreign to us, ours will also become more acceptable to you.

Just remember to judge us by our deeds.

The screens went black and in moments displayed their usual contents.

✂

Space observatories from across the globe had been contacted as well and all agreed to remain silent about the extraterrestrial contact until further information could be gathered. Doubt still remained about the authenticity of the message, but it began to dissipate when reports of miraculous recoveries from a host of illnesses surfaced.

"So it's happening," declared Casey, watching broadcasts from various countries at the SETI Institute.

As soon as she spoke, the monitors went blank and then a written message followed.

Greetings from Draco, as you now realize we have begun to rid your species of all maladies. This we do to prove our intention to liberate Earthlings of physical suffering. When our task is complete, we will be in further contact.

In the days that followed the great cure continued and the uninformed world was baffled. Theologians were among the first to speculate on the phenomenon, claiming their Gods had seen fit to end suffering. They put forth various explanations for this sudden show of grace. Most saw it as a form of divine intervention designed to purify humans before the end time. In the words of television evangelist Elmer Gantry the Third, "God has purged the pestilence from our bodies so that we may enter his kingdom as the immaculate children he created." The Pope concurred.

When there was no longer a trace of cancer, malaria, diabetes, or any other known disease on Earth, the Dracons transmitted a written message over all airwaves and Internet sites on the planet.

Dear Earthlings, we celebrate your health and are over-joyed that we have freed you of every infirmity known to your species. Please allow us to visit you and do not fear us because of our appearance.

While we will look very disturbing to you, there are species, also of goodwill, in other galaxies that would look far more horrifying.

Please know that you are not what we would regard as pleasant looking either. We will appear before you in our next transmission.

You may think we are very strange looking creatures, perhaps resembling what you know as arachnids. We assure you that we are not venomous.

At noon the next day, the Dracons made themselves visible to anyone with a screen. At first viewers were shocked by what they saw but after a lengthy and reassuring speech by Saglon Purt, most humans overcame their alarm. Subsequent transmissions by Dracons further mitigated the apprehension of Earth's inhabitants, who felt tremendous appreciation for the remarkable deed provided by the extraterrestrials.

In their last broadcast, the Dracons indicated that their ships would be landing the next day at several sites around the globe to make initial contact with Earthlings. They were true to their word, touching down in Egypt, Norway, India, Japan, United States, Spain, Kenya, and Australia as it became noon in each country. Once the Dracon ships had landed, their crews moved quickly through the awaiting crowds, causing some humans to panic and flee. As if equally frightened by the reaction of the Earthlings, the aliens swiftly returned to their vessels. Within moments the Draconian transporters lifted off and sped skyward, quickly vanishing from eyesight.

"What was that all about?" asked SETI's Casey Dwight, completely nonplussed by what she had just witnessed.

"They're already halfway across our solar system," commented Bill Wiley, staring at a monitor.

�֍

On the Dracon craft, there was intense discussion.

"Humans no longer have what we need. We have cured their ills and in so doing have inadvertently eliminated their capacity to secrete," observed Lord Cupleta, dourly.

"We attempted to reverse the process but failed," added the Deputy Chief, his furry head bowed.

"We must seek other opportunities," declared Cupleta. "Sadly there is no sustenance to be derived from Earthlings. We will not feed this day, and many humans will soon die from their inability to produce snot."

"Snot!" bellowed Saglon Purt, and his crew repeated the word over and over as saliva dripped from their mouths.

Language was not powerful enough to describe the phenomenon. — **CHARLES DICKENS**

RUBBED OUT

Following intense and often bitter debate involving town officials and local citizenry, the construction of the new Wal-Mart was approved by the slimmest of margins. The long-abandoned Gardner farm at the north end of Granby, New Hampshire, was to be the site of the giant box store. The house that stood in the overgrown field was so decrepit that it took only one push by a backhoe to make it collapse. In no time, everything but a small patch of dense foliage at the far edge of the property was cleared so construction could begin.

Things were going according to plan until several centuries-old tombstones were discovered within that thicket. Work was immediately halted while the state historic society conducted an investigation. Rubbings of the stones were taken and while there were no dates on the actual granite slabs, a date did appear in the lower corner of all six of the paper impressions—one that was three months in the future, *August 11, 2012.*

"Okay, let's do it again," said Corey Glenn to his assistant, Fran Kramer. "This didn't just happen, right?"

Again, the mysterious date appeared on the rubbings heightening the bafflement of the historical society's field researchers.

"This is really weird," observed Fran, staring in disbelief at the numbers on the rice paper.

"Weird? No, this is just plain freaky," replied Corwin. "Shoot me doing a rubbing with your cell. We need to document this or nobody is going to believe us."

When Corwin finished, both he and Fran reviewed the recording several times.

"Pictures don't lie. Damned if we didn't just experience a paranormal event, or whatever they call it."

"Whoa, this *is* really spooky," responded Fran, her eyes darting from the cell phone screen to the headstones.

"Now what?"

"We'll take everything back to the office and see what Billings has to say," answered Corwin, rolling up the rubbings. "Let's record this one more time to make sure we have it, okay? This time you do the rubbing, and I'll play cameraman."

✄

Back in Manchester, the director of the historical society, Lionel Billings, was as perplexed by the inexplicable event as were his two preservationists. Since their return to the office, the legal representatives of the box store chain had called demanding to know when construction could resume. Reluctantly Billings attempted to explain why further inquiry needed to be conducted at the site, but his words were met with skepticism, and the society was accused of deliberately delaying the project.

"C'mon. We got forty men on payroll and you're telling me they have to stand down because numbers are magically appearing on old tombstones. That's a bunch of voodoo crap. We got to get going here. Time is money," bellowed the box store's project chief.

Feeling pressured, Billings decided to go public about the Granby graveyard occurrence to gain more time to probe the phenomenon. But he never expected the brief account he gave to the *Manchester Chronicle* to create a firestorm. Almost immediately the national press jammed the society's phone lines and emails, and when Billings returned to the Granby site with Corey and Fran, they encountered a throng of television news trucks and reporters.

"Show us the invisible numbers," shouted several reporters, and Billings decided to oblige them.

"If this doesn't happen again, we're going to look damn ridiculous," he muttered to his colleagues. "Go ahead Corey. Do a rubbing. The cameras are rolling. This is your Hollywood moment."

Corey gathered his materials and went to the nearest headstone, his every move carefully chronicled by several video cameras.

"You can see there is no date on this monument. I'll now take a rubbing of its surface and you'll see what happens," announced Corey.

"Here goes nothing," whispered a worried Billings to Fran.

As Corey moved his lumberman's chalk against the paper at the bottom of the headstone, the now familiar date reappeared.

"It says *August 11, 2012*," observed a reporter, causing a wave of murmurs among his cohorts.

"Thank God," sighed Billings, patting Fran on the shoulder. "But how the hell is this happening?"

A long round of questions from the assembled reporters followed the demonstration. All three members of the historical society continued to be at a loss to provide a plausible explanation for the appearance of the date on the rubbing.

"Sorry, but we just don't know what's going on here. As you can see, there's no date on the stones, but one appears when a rubbing is done. Perhaps one of you would like to try it?" inquired Billings.

"I'll do it," responded a woman Lionel recognized from a local television station.

"Great! Fran, give her a hand, would you?"

"Sure," she replied, holding a piece of rice paper against a different headstone and instructing the reporter how to move the chalk against it.

"Oh my God, there it is!" exclaimed the newsperson as the cryptic alphanumeric symbols appeared. "Is this some kind of trick paper?"

"No ma'am. It's standard Aqaba gravestone rubbing paper. If you have a regular piece of paper, you can try it," responded Billings.

"I do," said the reporter, tearing a sheet from her notebook.

"Go ahead, Karen...rub it."

"You know my name?" responded the correspondent as she moved the chalk across the paper.

"Watch you on the news," answered Billings.

As soon as the first few letters of the date appeared, the gathering rumbled in astonishment.

"This is...*amazing*. What does it mean? The date must have some significance!" exclaimed the dumbfounded reporter.

"Like I said, we're as much in the dark about it as you are, but we're going to continue our investigation of the site in hopes of coming up with some answers," offered Billings.

❧

That evening the local media, as well as the national networks, carried accounts of the incident unfolding in Granby. By the next day the number of reporters at the cemetery had increased three-fold and police had to cordon off the area. By week's end, media from across the globe had descended on the small community. Droves of curiosity-seekers showed up as well. Inundated by requests for information, the historical society held a news conference, headlined by the state's lieutenant governor, Max Harrington.

"At this point, Mr. Billings and his staff continue to investigate this unusual occurrence. A team of paranormal experts and forensic specialists will join them in an attempt to solve this mystery. Mr. Billings, would you like to add anything?" inquired Harrington.

"*Ah*, not really. I think you've pretty well covered...*things*," replied Billings, stepping away from the microphone.

The lieutenant governor watched Billings as he receded to the background and then he added, "Well, okay. I guess that's it. We'll let you know what's going on as soon as we know, er...what's going on. Thank you."

"What the hell else can I say about this thing? Maybe we need to bring in David Copperfield," mumbled Billings into Corey's ear.

The crowd at the site increased substantially each day as teams of investigators from a host of universities and government agencies attempted to discover the secret of the Granby apparition. As the weeks passed, nothing was resolved, but great speculation as to its meaning flooded the Internet and airwaves. Most were apocalyptic in nature. August 11, 2012 was declared the new *End Time,* and millions of people around the globe were preparing for it.

Meanwhile, national leaders attempted to mitigate the fears of their citizens, but reason was supplanted by growing panic and in many places order began to breakdown. There were skeptics, but the incomprehensible manifestation of the headstone's date was proof enough for most of the planet's inhabitants that Earth's days were numbered. Even *The New York Times* proclaimed, "This one is different," concluding that no prediction of Armageddon was ever preceded by such a mystifying and supernatural communiqué.

In an effort to disburse the vast crowds that had flocked to Granby, state officials decided to remove the headstones from their site. The town had run out of food and other essentials and locals were in a dither. When authorities appeared to dig up the gravestones, they were met with opposition. The multitudes surrounded the half dozen state workers and threatened to harm them if they so much as touched the ground around what it termed the "sacred markers." Fearing for their lives, the would-be gravediggers quickly threw down their shovels and departed.

By the time the sun rose on August 11, 2012, in Granby, the world had experienced a level of lawlessness and chaos never before seen. As the appointed time unfolded, the civil unrest subsided, and as it approached midnight on what most of the world's population believed was doomsday, crowds gathered in city squares and parks and waited for human existence to end. But it did not. The hands of the clock continued to move, and it became August 12, 2012. Conceiving that it was just another false prophecy, the assembled masses breathed a sigh of relief and returned to the routine of their lives.

Fifty light-years away on Gliese 667, six trillion spectators—watching eight hundred ten-mile long JumboTron screens—roared with pleasure at the finale of "Galaxy Gotcha'," a reality show presented by the Office of Giliesian Amusement. In the Imperial Stadium, the viewers chanted "More! More!" with their limbs outstretched toward their monarch. King Groidro Phrobe rose and signaled for silence with his six glimmering appendages.

"You wish more? Then *more* you shall have," proclaimed the king, pointing his royal scepters in the direction of Earth.

At the Granby graveyard, the crowds had departed, leaving only Billings, Corey, and Fran. They had returned in the off chance that something might have changed when they took a *post*-August 11, 2012 rubbing.

"*What the…?*" exclaimed Billings, as his chalk moved across the bottom of a headstone revealing a new inscription—*November 14, 2012.*

On Giliese 667, the cheers of satisfaction were deafening.

It is in fantasy that the real live.

— ANONYMOUS

WHAT THE SEA BRINGS

Merchant ships transporting cargo and personnel across the Atlantic to U.S. allies during World War Two were all too often torpedoed off the East Coast. This was the fate of the *Chatham* carrying ensign Wayne Harley. His body washed ashore in a remote rocky cove on the northern Maine coast. There it remained unseen for days until sixteen-year old Caitlin Bosworth found it.

It was the happiest day of her life.

Caitlin had suffered from oxygen deprivation during birth and consequently had the mental acumen of some-one half her age. She had a sweet temperament and de-rived great pleasure playing along the shoreline that her house faced. Her parents adored their only child and did everything to make her life cheerful and as intellectually stimulating as possible. It was their greatest hope that Caitlin would one day reach a level of proficiency that would allow her to live independent of their constant oversight.

However, Caitlin's doctor was not optimistic about her chances of living on her own. He had told the Bosworths that their daughter's mind would likely remain at the level of a ten-year old through her adulthood. In other words, they would have to care for her the balance of their lives or institutionalize her, which was something they would never consider doing. The joy they got from her existence more than balanced the burden involved in raising a de-velopmentally challenged daughter. She was the delight of their lives and the prospect of having a child who would remain a child forever was far from unpleasant.

One of the things Caitlin loved most was hearing the romantic fairy tales her parents read to her. Beyond that, she also loved listening to the radio. Among a host of programs, she got the most pleasure from the dramatic stories on *Lux Radio Theater*. One about a prince who falls in love with a peasant girl particularly captured her fancy.

"I will marry a prince. A handsome prince," she declared after the program.

✂

In the coming days it was all Caitlin thought about, and her mother and father happily played along with her.

"You are *our* beautiful princess," they said as she swirled around in her favorite frock.

Caitlin continued her ecstatic dance out of the house to play in the bright early autumn sun.

"Come back soon for lunch, honey!" shouted her mother.

A report on the radio caught Lyle Bosworth's attention. "Krauts sunk another ship not far away. Around a hundred sailors on her," he reported to his wife.

"The poor parents of those boys," said Sarah Bosworth, staring out the window at her daughter. "To lose a child is the worse thing I can imagine. We're so lucky to have our little girl."

Caitlin soon reached the spot where she spent so many happy hours lost in her imaginary world. It was there that Wayne Harley washed up. When Caitlin saw the young man's body she was instantly enthralled.

"My prince. You've come for me, haven't you?"

"Yes, my princess. I *have* come for you," she heard him answer.

Caitlin ran to where his body sat.

"I *knew* you would come. Do you want some tea? You look so cold."

She remained with the drowned seaman until her mother's distant voice caught her attention.

"It's time for lunch. Please don't leave. I'll come back soon and bring you some food."

As soon as Caitlin returned home, she reported her encounter to her parents. They had heard many fantastical accounts from her before and always listened to them with great affection and interest.

"He is very handsome, but he is tired after his long journey from his castle. May I bring him a sandwich? He is very hungry."

Of course you may, darling. Maybe he would like a piece of cake, too."

"Yes, mommy. He likes sweets."

Caitlin ran quickly to her waiting prince and then placed as much food into his open mouth as would fit.

"You're so hungry! Mommy said you would like her cake."

"It is the most delicious cake I have ever eaten," replied Caitlin's prince.

"Where is your castle?"

"Across the sea."

"Will we live there?"

"Yes, forever."

"Is there a beautiful garden?"

"There is none better in any kingdom."

"My favorite flower is the red rose."

""It is the flower of my realm. You will always have them for your hair."

The entranced couple conversed until the sun neared the horizon.

"I must go home or my parents will worry. I'll come back in the morning with mommy's biscuits. You will love them as much as her cake."

⁂

Over the next several days, Caitlin spent long rapturous hours in conversation with the dead seaman. They spoke of many extraordinary things, all based on their future life together.

Caitlin had had many imaginary friends before, but her parents could not recall any that so absorbed her.

"Do you think she's okay? Every waking moment she talks about this prince. It is all so real to her."

" I wouldn't worry, honey," Lyle replied to his wife. "She has a vivid imagination. You know that. Doctor Fairfield said that special children like her sometimes do. It's kind of a gift, really."

"I guess you're right."

"As long as she's happy. That's the main thing."

Exhilarated by her extraordinary new experience Caitlin rose before sunrise and eagerly waited in the kitchen for her mother to appear.

"Good morning, sweetheart. What would you like for breakfast this morning?"

"He loves your biscuits, mommy. Make biscuits."

"It's raining out, so you better wait until it stops before you go to your friend."

"My prince, you mean, mommy."

"Yes, of course, your prince."

"But he will be terribly hungry. Please, I can wear my pretty raincoat. See, mommy, it's not raining very hard," observed Caitlin, looking out of the kitchen window.

Mrs. Bosworth reluctantly gave in to her daughter's plea in return making her promise to come back quickly.

❈

When Caitlin reached the cove she found her beloved lying on his side as waves washed over his legs.

"Wake up, my dear prince. I have your biscuits."

When he did not move, she exerted all her strength to raise his body, leaning it against the rock upon which it had rested.

"There, now. Here, eat your breakfast," she said, placing pieces of biscuits into his frozen maw. "I must go home until the rain stops. I promised mommy, but I'll come back later."

"Please stay with me," she heard her prince say.

"But mommy will be worried."

"You *are* my princess now. Your mother will understand. We will soon go to my castle."

"Yes...yes, I *am* your princess, so I *will* stay with you," said Caitlin, placing a soft kiss on the corpse's cold cheek.

As time passed, Sarah Bosworth grew concerned, especially since it was raining harder and the wind had picked up. She decided she had to find her daughter.

"I'm coming with you," said her husband.

As they left the house they were surprised and disheartened by how ferocious the weather had become.

"Let's go to the cove first," suggested Sarah, knowing it was her daughter's favorite place to play.

When they reached the tiny inlet, the sky had cleared.

"That is so odd," remarked Lyle. "I have never seen a storm pass so quickly."

"Look, it's her raincoat!" exclaimed Sarah, dashing to where it floated in the nearby surf.

"Caitlin! Where *are* you?" they called frantically, their voices echoing in the deserted cove.

A pity beyond all telling
Is hid in the heart of love.

— **W.B. YEATS**

A PERFECT MATCH

Kidney failure can result in a host of symptoms, among them frequent urination, swelling in the limbs, constant fatigue, skin rash, ammonia breath, nausea, dizziness, and lower back pain. Ellen Herbert experienced all of the aforementioned, as well as the chills. Although the thermostat in her house was raised to nearly eighty degrees on what was a balmy spring day, she still felt cold. Her misery index, as she called it, had reached an all time high, and she clung to the hope that Thursday would arrive quickly. It was then that she would receive a healthy kidney from her husband and life would return to normal, which it had not been for the past two years.

Despite Ellen's battle with a potentially fatal illness, the fates had not been entirely unkind to her. It turned out that her husband's extra kidney could serve as a replacement for her failing one. There was not a moment's hesitation on Brian Herbert's part to give up one of his organs for the woman he loved more than anything. The thought of living without her was inconceivable, so he considered himself blessed when he was told he was her perfect match.

"I knew I was all along," said Brian, patting his wife's hand.

"It's a lot to give someone, especially with your heart condition," replied Ellen, smiling wanly.

"The doctor said it is *not* an issue, and you're not just someone. You're my soul mate."

When the day finally arrived for their mutual surgeries, the Herberts were in the best mood they had been in for a very long time. The idea that their dark days would soon be a thing of the past lifted their spirits—spirits that had sunk to subterranean levels when Ellen had been diagnosed with renal failure.

Prepped and on their way to surgery, the Herberts held hands as their respective gurneys were rolled down the hospital corridor side-by-side. Five days later, their operations a success, they were moved in tandem in wheel chairs to the hospital's main entrance. Ellen felt better than she had in two years, and Brian felt the same as he had upon entering the hospital. Life soon returned to normal.

Nine months after the transplant life took a devastating turn for Brian. The love of his life informed him she was leaving him for another man. With considerable solemnity, Ellen informed her husband that she had fallen in love with someone else.

"I'm so sorry. After all you did for me, I feel terrible. But I can't deny what I feel for David," uttered Ellen, looking off into the distance.

"Why? What did I ever do to deserve this? David? Who is he?"

"You did nothing to deserve this. You've always been wonderful to me," replied Ellen, still looking away. "David is someone I met at the gym. It's crazy, I know. I never expected this to happen. He's younger, and..."

"Jesus, this can't be for real. We've been happily married for fourteen years," protested Brian, beginning to hyperventilate.

"I haven't been happy in the last few years. Even before I got sick. It wasn't you. I've always felt like I was missing something in life. Then there was the kidney failure, and I thought I was going to die. But then I didn't, and I met..."

"David...yeah, you said that. Well, why don't you take my kidney and leave if you're so in love."

"I didn't mean to hurt you, Brian. I love you. I'm just not *in* love with you. I'll leave and get an apartment. You should stay in the house. I can't take care of it. You know me."

"I thought I *did* know you, but boy was I wrong," said Brian, wiping the tears from his cheeks.

Within an hour, Ellen had packed and departed, leaving Brian alone and anguished. For several days he remained home and cut off from the world. The phone rang incessantly, but Brian hardly noticed curled up as he was under layers of bed covers. Four days after Ellen's apocryphal announcement, there was a ceaseless ringing of his doorbell. Reluctantly, he climbed from bed—still in the clothes he had worn on the day his life had been turned upside down—and dragged his body to the door.

His sister Alice stood in the doorway staring at him. "Brian, what's happened to you? Where's Ellen? You look awful. What's the problem?"

Suddenly Brian felt light-headed and staggered to the closest chair.

"Did you take your heart pill?" asked Alice, looking at him anxiously.

"I'm okay. Well...maybe *not* okay exactly," muttered Brian, tears welling up in his eyes.

"Where's Ellen? What's going on?"

"Ellen's left me," answered Brian.

"*Huh?* What do you mean she *left* you?"

"She found someone else and moved out."

"You're joking. Ellen wouldn't do that to you. She loves you."

"She loves me, but she's not *in* love with me. She's *in* love with David."

"David?"

"Her boyfriend. Some guy she met at the gym"

Brian proceeded to give his sister the details. After he filled her in, the siblings sat silently for several minutes—Brian shaking his head abjectly and his sister staring out the window in disbelief.

"You gave her your kidney, for Christ's sake," said Alice, breaking the long silence.

"I gave her my heart, too," moaned Brian, dabbing the moisture from the corners of his eyes.

After another week of trying to regain his emotional footing, Brian returned to work but said nothing about his breakup to his fellow agents at Boswell Realty. Despite Brian's putting on a game face, his colleagues sensed that something was not right. The one person at work whom Brian considered a close friend was Kathleen Boswell, the mother of the man who owned the agency. The elder Boswell served as the receptionist for her son's business and was well liked by everyone, especially Brian. She reminded him of his own mother, who had died when he was only nine.

"You sure are mopey lately, Brian? I know sales are way down, but you're not alone in this economy," offered Kathleen, when Brian barely acknowledged her on his way to his desk.

"Sorry, my mind is far away these days," replied Brian.

"Now why is that?"

Brain decided to reveal the cause of his gloom but did so cryptically, reciting a piece of verse he had memorized when he came across it on a website devoted to betrayed spouses.

"*'I rage, I melt, I burn. The feeble woman has stabbed me to the heart.'*"

"What?" asked Kathleen, baffled by Brian's soliloquy.

"Ellen's left me," blurted Brian, histrionically.

"Stop it! You're acting bizarre."

"Yes, I am acting bizarre, but I'm also telling the truth. My wife fell in love with her Pilates instructor."

"She really left you?"

"Don't tell anybody, please. I'm telling you because I know you won't blab it all over, and you're a good friend."

"Oh, I'm *so* sorry, Brian. I thought you two were rock solid."

"I did, too. I still can't believe it. It's like having a knife in my heart...or back," said Brian, his voice cracking.

"This *will* get better. You're a great guy. There are plenty of women that would find you very attractive. I still can't believe Ellen would do this after everything you've done for her. My God, you gave her your liver."

"My kidney. You die without a liver, so you've got to keep the only one you have. Although, she may as well have taken my liver."

"Of course, your *kidney*," replied Kathleen, with an embarrassed chuckle. "Anyway, this too shall pass. Everything does. What is it they say, 'What doesn't kill you makes you stronger?'"

That's exactly what Alice had said, thought Brian, bidding Kathleen goodbye as he headed to his desk.

"Stay strong, Brian," blurted Kathleen, as he rounded the corner and disappeared from view.

✂

Despite his desperate efforts to get over Ellen, the pain of her departure remained no less excruciating to him even six months later. It was all he could do to keep from throwing in the towel and leaping off a bridge. Then he received news that might have cheered a lesser man. The kidney he had donated to his ex-wife was rejecting her.

"Well, if that's not poetic justice, I don't know what is. Serves her right," responded Alice, surprised that the news did nothing to lift her brother's spirits.

"I feel badly about it."

"Why? She ruined your life," protested Alice.

"It's my kidney that's failing."

"You *are* hopeless. The woman takes a piece of your body and then runs off with another man, and *you're* feeling guilty? Brother mine, I think she took your brains, too. C'mon, there's no way you should feel anything but payback for the way she treated you."

Brian's concern for his wife deepened when he heard that her young lover had abandoned her in her moment of need. Despite the insistence of Alice and Kathleen that he ignore Ellen's plight, Brian could not help but go to her aid. His feelings for her held his actions captive.

"Brian!" exclaimed Ellen, upon seeing him at her door. "You're the last person I expected to see."

"I heard you weren't doing so well," said Brian, shocked by her diminished appearance.

"Well, that should be obvious," replied Ellen, staring up at him from her wheel chair.

"No, you look fine. It's good to see you."

"Please come in. Sorry about the mess. I haven't had much strength to keep things tidy. I hope you're not here to gloat, although I can understand if that's why you came by."

"Just wanted to see if you needed anything," said Brian, feeling a sudden surge of affection for the woman he continued to love despite what had happened.

"I can't tell you how sorry for what I did. What a bitch I've been. Believe me, I never meant this to happen. I don't know why it did. It wasn't that I didn't love you."

"Yeah, I know, you just weren't *in* love with me," offered Brian, downcast.

"Frankly, I don't even know what that means anymore. I acted like a love struck teenager with David. My head was all screwed up. I couldn't see what I was doing, and you were caught in the crossfire of my stupidity. It wasn't long after I left you that I realized my mistake."

"You said you were in love with David," Brian reminded Ellen.

"I was infatuated…temporarily insane, maybe. I've always loved you, Brian. Now I can see it was the *real* thing, not what I had with David. Can you ever forgive me?"

"If you can you forgive me for giving you a bum kidney?" said Brian, touching Ellen's cheek.

"Everything you gave me was good. I was just too foolish to recognize that before it was too late."

※

Over the coming weeks, Brian did everything he could to make life better for his ailing wife, but he knew her days were numbered. Doctors had not found another matching kidney and her treatments were becoming less and less effective. When it was obvious the end was approaching for Ellen, Brian decided to move her back in their house. This he did to the consternation of Alice, who vowed not to visit him as long as Ellen was living with him.

"I'm sorry, I just can't deal with your letting her move back in here," barked Alice, stomping out of the house.

As she had climbed into her car and drove off, Brian fell unconscious, having suffered a massive coronary. Several days later when he finally regained consciousness, he was given startling news by the attending cardiologist.

"You got a new heart. It was the only way you would survive."

"I had a transplant?" asked Brian incredulously, his voice barely more than a whisper.

"You were very lucky. Fate intervened in a most extraordinary way. A heart became available just at the moment you needed it. I know this is something that will come as a shock to you, but your wife gave you her heart."

"I know she did," replied Brian, his mind still clouded.

"No, Mr. Herbert, *literally*. She gave you *her* heart."

For many days, my brain
Worked with a dim and undetermined sense
Of unknown modes of being.
                    —WILLIAM WORDSWORTH

Mmmna

The first time Amy heard the odd sound she ignored it. The second time, however, it aroused her curiosity, and she looked out the window. Yet nothing in the yard appeared different or out of place. *But how* would *it look if the source of the sound had been there?* she wondered. It was an unidentifiable noise, nothing she could associate with anything she knew—a sort of half-human, half-mechanical interjection into the early evening stillness.

Amy attempted to reproduce the peculiar sound. "*Urrra*...no, *ennna*, nope...*Vrrra.*" She pursed her lips and tried again. "*Mmma.* Almost. *Mmmma.* Yeah, that's it... *Mmmna.*"

As Amy stepped back from the window, satisfied that she had replicated what she thought she was hearing, she heard it again. This time it seemed to come from inside the condo. *Weird*, she thought, carefully checking the kitchen and bedroom.

"*Mmmna*," came the otherworldly utterance.

The bathroom. It must be coming from the bathroom.

With growing trepidation, Amy moved down the hall to where she was certain the sound originated. She slowly pushed the door open and flicked the light switch.

Nothing there! "Come out, come out, wherever you are," sang Amy.

"*Mmmna …*"

Shit! It has to be inside the apartment, but where is it? What is it? Amy pondered, continuing her search. As she inspected the kitchen and bathroom cupboards and the hall and bedroom closets, the mysterious din continued, though it appeared to be growing louder. After probing virtually every corner of her house, she collapsed on her couch. *Maybe the sound is only in my head, but I'm sure I took my meds.*

"*Mmmna…*"

In a sudden panic, Amy leapt to her feet. *What am I going to do? Call my mother.* She hit the speed dial on her cell. After two rings, "*Mmmna.*" After four more rings, another "*Mmmna.*" No answer. *Where is she? Where is she?* Amy whimpered.

She sat back down and calculated how much time elapsed between the haunting orations. She counted four beats between each. *My sister. I'll call Kim.* "*Mmmna …Mmmna…Mmmna.*" No answer. *Where the hell is she? Oh, God, where is anybody?*

Amy hit the button on the TV remote. Dr. Phil blurted "*Mmmna*" to a young, teary-eyed woman seated across from him. "*Mmmna,*" she answered. Amy tossed the remote across the room, and pressed speed dial again. "*Mmmna…*" She threw the phone in the direction she had thrown the remote and began to sob. *Why is this happening?* she repeated over and over again.

Then came a knock on her door. Amy ran to answer it. In the dim light of the hallway she could make out her mother and sister.

"Thank, God!" she cried and extended her arms to embrace them.

"Mmmna," they said in unison, reaching out to Amy. *"Mmmna..."*

Mother and sister took hold of Amy's trembling hands and guided her down to the building's entrance. Along the way other tenants joined them—all chanting *"Mmmna ..."* A feeling of peace began to envelop Amy, and she joined in what was no longer a bizarre aural intrusion but now seemed a soothing mantra.

When they reached the street, they joined a throng of others intoning *"Mmmna."*

The swaying crowd looked upward toward the vast shadows that were blocking the stars.

In headaches and in worry

Vaguely life leaks away.

— W.H. Auden

A Certain Future

"Hey, man, I'm a decaying body in a year," snapped Jason, after a friend had asked him for his thoughts on how global warming would change the world.

"I'm sorry, dude," responded Marty. "I forgot. You look so healthy and strong."

"On the *outside*. Inside the walls are crumbling."

Marty was about to say something but changed his mind.

"Chill, man. I'm good with it. I mean there's not a freaking thing I can do about it. Better off than the rest of humanity though. You guys got to fret about what's ahead for you. No fretting about that for me. I know exactly what the future holds."

"Isn't there some kind of experimental drug or treatment you can get? Some clinical trial going on?"

"Been down that road already. Did more Googling and emailing about it than you could imagine. Call me Mr. Due Diligence. Nothing can stop those hungry little brain eaters from emptying out this cupboard," said Jason, tapping his temple.

"It's a *Gloma*-something tumor, you said."

A *Glioblastoma Multiforme*, to be exact. It usually affects older people. Guess I'm just lucky."

"Some luck," mumbled Marty, shaking his head. "You're sure cool about this. I'd be a real mess."

"Hey, think about it. I've been *liberated*."

"Huh? What do you mean?"

"What worries you about the future, Marty?"

"Stuff...*things*."

"Like, will you lose your job? Will your wife cheat on you? Will your kid get run over? Will your parents move in with you? Will you get audited? Will your house catch fire? Will you get robbed...?"

"Okay, I get the idea."

"Will an asteroid hit Earth? Will there be another terrorist attack? Will you be paralyzed? Will you get dementia...?"

Marty looked at his watch and stood up. "Whoa, got to get back to work."

"Will you get cancer? Yeah, that's a good one to worry about. I don't have to worry about that one."

"Good point, Jason. Look, I'm..."

"How about erectile dysfunction? Now that's a concern to keep you up at night...no pun intended. Hey, maybe a shooter in your workplace? That one could happen anytime, right? Then there's a possible global pandemic and that cliff might break apart in the Azores causing a killer tsunami right here."

"Ah yes, there's *that*. Well, I'll see you soon, buddy," blurted Marty, turning and hurrying out of the restaurant.

That guy is one lucky bastard, he thought, climbing into his car.

[His] words were like tinfoil; they shone and they covered things up. —**HELEN CROSS**

OVER THE BORDER

Emil Bonner was certain he had written a masterful novel—a narrative tour de force. But American publishers did not appear to share his view, or so it seemed from the dozen rejection slips he had received over the past year of searching for a press. *They don't even have the common decency to send a personal note,* he sulked. To date he'd received only the standard turndown, usually in postcard form. He was consoled by his writer girlfriend, Amanda, if not by anyone else. Most of his handful of friends had tired of his constant lament to the point they had begun to avoid him. On the other hand, Amanda reminded him that some great novels had been rejected countless times. She had Googled to come up with a list of authors who had faced a similar plight.

"Hon, you've only received a dozen rejection slips. You can't lose faith. It's a great book. I know it. I read it twice."

"A dozen is a *lot*," grumbled Emil.

"Well, one of your favorite books, *Zen and the Art of Motorcycle Maintenance,* was rejected one hundred and twenty-one times."

"No way!"

"And Stephen King's *Carrie* was turned down thirty times before his wife, Tabitha, fished it out of the trash and told him not to give up on it."

"Yeah, but..."

"*Gone with the Wind* was rejected thirty-eight times and James Joyce's *Dubliners* was sent out two-dozen times with no takers."

"How do you know all this?

"My degree is in English, silly. You know that."

"Mine is, too, but I didn't realize . . ."

"*Jonathan Livingston Seagull* was refused eighteen times and..."

"Okay, okay! I get it. I'll check out some more places to send it, but I really think it's a lost cause.

❀

After lunch Emil went online to the publisher directories he had bookmarked. Among his favorite was one called Duotrope. It offered one-stop shopping for every type of fiction and non-fiction writing. He had used it to place a half-dozen short stories in webzines and wondered how it could continue its excellent services to writers free of charge. So impressed was Emil with the exceptional author's resource, he donated $25.00 toward its continuing existence. The idea that it might fold disturbed him since he could see how valuable it might be to him in the future.

Under the category of romantic novels, which was where his book best fit, he found a publisher that looked particularly promising. Its mission statement corresponded with his notion of what a press should aspire to.

Heart Books is seeking original works of literature. We do not publish the predictable or formulaic. We seek novels with contemporary characters and fresh, believable plots. A manuscript should possess strong and natural dialog and plausible character interaction. Anything less will not be considered. Writers should be certain that all description is authentic and indicative of period and place. Heart Books is particularly receptive to exciting new voices in the romance genre. We seek to add serious and unique titles to our expanding catalog…

Yes! thought Emil. *Yes! This is the one.*

As he read on he believed he had finally found the ideal place to submit his novel. Everything seemed to suggest that Heart Books would be receptive to what he had achieved, until he read the last sentence on the publisher's guidelines page.

We only consider submissions from women of Canadian origin.

"Shit!" he muttered, pushing his chair back from his desk. "It figures."

Then Emil had an idea. *Why not submit his novel using a woman's name? At least he might get a response… maybe some useful comments or words of encouragement,* he considered. Believing he had nothing to lose and feeling mounting frustration with the whole publisher search process, Emil decided to do it. *What about a name?* he pondered, and then decided to use his girlfriend's moniker—*keep it in the family, at least.* Adding to the appeal of his choice was the fact that she had grown up in Toronto—*a Canadian woman.*

Emil decided against asking Amanda for permission to use her name, figuring it really didn't matter all that much, since he would likely never hear back from the press or just get the usual "no thank you" note. Moreover, his girlfriend might object on the basis of principle. She had an almost stoic, if not rigid, approach to things, no matter how small, that smacked of dishonesty. While Emil admired this quality in her, he sometimes viewed it as a bit puritanical. It had been the source of friction in their relationship on more than one occasion.

"That's not very nice," was Amanda's pat rejoinder when Emil said something she perceived as sarcastic or cynical.

She had nearly flipped out when Emil confessed that he had accidentally dented a car while he was parking and then sped away to avoid an insurance claim.

"Whose side are you on?" he exclaimed.

To which she had snapped, "On the *side* of honesty."

She had spoken in a tone that reminded him of his mother when she would reprimand him for some not so infrequent lapse in moral judgment.

No, I'll keep this to myself. If they want my novel, then I'll deal with it. Otherwise, it never happened, thought Emil, as he downloaded his magnum opus to the publisher. In his cover letter, he assumed his girlfriend's persona indicating that he had grown up in Toronto with parents who were true-blue Canadians. *That should be enough to get past their damn requirements.*

Soon after submitting *Star Roses* to Heart Books, Emil had all but forgotten he'd done so. For the next few weeks he continued to send out his manuscript and receive the customary rejection notices. Meanwhile, as the two went on with their daily lives, Amanda continued work on her own novel about the search for a lost Ojibwa girl in Saskatchewan in the early 1900s.

Emil tried to appear interested in his girlfriend's novel but was far more consumed by the fate of his own fictional work to really engage her on the subject. This bothered Amanda but she kept quiet about the hurt she felt trying hard to offer Emil as much support as he appeared to need, which was substantial. He had a delicate ego that needed considerable massaging to keep him in an agreeable mood. To Amanda, keeping him in good spirits was worth the effort. When he wasn't brooding about the fate of his novel, he was decent company, and they shared enough common interests to keep the relationship viable.

A month after Emil had sent his manuscript to Heart Books he received an email that at first made him cheer out loud and then sink into his chair in despair.

Dear Amanda,

It is with great pleasure that we offer you a contract for your excellent novel *Star Roses*. We find it fresh and original and believe it will compliment our list of forthcoming titles. Please see the attached contract. If you find it agreeable, sign and return it to us within the next fourteen days.

My very best regards…and *congratulations!*

Lyle Carson

Senior Acquisitions Editor

Oh my God! They want to publish my book but not with my name, sighed Emil, staring in disbelief at the email. *I don't believe it! I just don't believe it! I'll withdraw it. Send back the contract. My life is a freaking horror story.*

But Emil could not bring himself to pass up the opportunity to see his words in print, even if they would be attributed to someone else. At least his girlfriend's name would be on it and not the name of a total stranger, he rationalized, but then he thought about Amanda's reaction to being a part of the deception. *She'll go postal on me… freak out.*

After several more minutes of agonizing over the situation, he decided to sign the contract, figuring the tiny Canadian publisher would only put out a modest run of the book and it would fade into obscurity with Amanda never knowing about its existence. *At least,* Star Roses *will be published. No one wants it in this country. That's for sure.*

Dear Mr. Carson,

I'm thrilled that my novel will be published by Heart Books. I have read the contract and agree to its terms. It is attached to this email. I look forward to my book's publication with great excitement.

Sincerely,

Amanda Gale

❀

While Amanda toiled on her novel, Emil began work on another. Three months after his initial correspondence with Lyle Carson, he received the page proof of *Star Roses*. Little editing had been required, and he quickly made the suggested revisions and returned the manuscript via email. Five months later, almost to the day that Amanda completed her first novel, *The Disappearance of Little Deer*, Emil found a package addressed to his girlfriend from Heart Books in a Fed Ex envelope inside the lobby door of their apartment building. He was thankful he had the chance to snatch it up before she saw it.

Rather than take the chance of Amanda seeing it, he walked to the nearby park where he opened the envelope and extracted the object it held. It was an oversize paperback with a matt finish cover depicting a starry sky intersected by two red roses. Thumbing through the book's pages, Emil was thrilled to see his words in print, but his delight was short-lived when he remembered that he could never take public credit for its appearance.

He rose from the park bench and deposited the book in a nearby trashcan. As soon as he did, he had second thoughts and fished it out of the barrel. He took it home and stashed it behind a bookcase in his office space. During the coming weeks, no matter where he was, at work or home, he could not shake the image of the book's cover from his mind's eye. However, eventually it began to fade as he dove deeper into his new manuscript, which he was beginning to believe superior to *Star Roses*.

"Another rejection," noted Amanda, holding a postcard in her hand.

To date, she had received a half-dozen turndowns on her first novel, but unlike her boyfriend, she had received a couple of brief, but encouraging, notes from editors that helped buoy her outlook.

"No personal note this time, huh?" asked Emil.

"Nope. Just your standard rejection," replied Amanda. "But I sent it to a couple of other publishers, so, as I've told you, hope springs eternal and good things eventually happen."

Her positive attitude grated on Emil because he felt she was out-of-touch with the harsh realities of getting a book into print without going the route of a vanity press or eBook.

"You've just started. It's a long tough road ahead. The odds are against you no matter how good your stuff is. The book market is crashing, so don't hold your breath."

"You're just down because you haven't had any luck with your own yet, but you will."

"I don't think it's about luck. It has more to do with *who* you are than what you *write.*"

"What do you mean, '*who* you are'?"

"Nothing…never mind," pouted Emil, rising and returning to his computer.

❊

Encouraged by how well his work was going on his new novel, Emil's mood began to improve and the tension with Amanda decreased. Occasionally he received emails from Heart Books describing what it was doing to get word out about the release of *Star Roses*, which struck Emil as modest at best. *Who cares,* he thought. *Let it die. It's been nothing but a sad experience.* To Emil the frustrating episode was all but closed.

He was wrong…terribly wrong…

"What the hell is this?" said Amanda, waving an envelope and its contents in her hand.

She had just returned from grocery shopping and had picked up the mail on her way up to their apartment.

"Huh? What's the matter?" asked Emil, thrown by her anger.

"An award for *my* book? What's this about?" said Amanda, heaving the letter at Emil.

He picked it up from the floor and read it.

Dear Amanda,

We are thrilled to inform you that your marvelous book, *Star Roses*, has won the prestigious Canadian First Book Award. It will be presented in Vancouver on May 22 and Heart Books will be delighted to sponsor your attendance. This means a great deal to your reputation as an author and to the sales of your book, which will certainly reflect the significance of this stellar recognition.

Congratulations,
Lyle Carson

"I'm sorry. I should have told you. I didn't think it would get to this point, honestly."

"Told me what? This is *your* book but *my* name on it. Why did you do that?"

"I never thought publication would happen. It was a momentary impulse. They had this restriction that only Canadian women could submit to them, and I was frustrated because otherwise they seemed just right for my book. So I sent it to them with your name on it. Stupid, I know, but they accepted *Star Roses,* and I thought, why not. We could make a few dollars. I should have told you I put your name on the manuscript."

"Damn right you should have told me. You deceived the publisher and stole my name in the process. That's fraud...a crime."

"Only if you make it a crime. C'mon. Who's to know? You know how goddamn hard it is to get a book published. You can use this to get your own book published. It'll give you a step up. Besides, how have I gained from this? My book is credited to someone else . . . *you*. So get off your high horse and stop treating me like a common thief. I never meant this to happen. It was just..."

"An unethical act? I don't know about you...*us*. This really changes things."

"I said I was sorry. Look, submit your novel to Heart under your own name. They'll take it. After *Star Roses* won the award, you're good as gold with them."

"I'm not going to accept an award for something I didn't write."

"How many rejections have you gotten for your book so far? Look, don't be silly. This could be the break you need. It's miserable out there. Real publishers are disappearing, and the ones that remain only want guaranteed bestsellers. We don't write that kind of book. Heart would be perfect for you. I'm not getting anything out of this.

It's not like I did this to benefit myself. I did it as an experiment, and, well, it won an award. At least I know I can write. That's all I get out of this, but you can get so much more."

"I got to think this thing out. I need some air. I'm going to take a walk."

An hour later Amanda returned, and her mood had changed.

"Okay, what if I do accept the award. What then? What about you?"

"What about me? Just do the smart thing. Get your own manuscript published. Maybe I'll come with you and meet the staff at Heart Books. You could help me a little if you'd acknowledge me during your acceptance speech. Maybe say that as a writer myself I helped you sharpen *Star Roses,* or that I inspired you to finish it. Something like that could open the door for me at Heart."

"So you want me to accept an award I didn't earn and praise you for helping me win it?"

"Well, not exactly like that. Jeez, we're a team, right? We're both trying to get our books published, and you know that isn't easy. This could get us both on track. It could be great. Just what we need for our careers."

After a long silence, Amanda said what Emil prayed she would. "I'll think about it."

"Great! And I am sorry I didn't tell you about putting your name on my novel. I should have, but this is turning out to be a good thing."

"Yeah, a good *thing*," said Amanda, with a note of sarcasm in her voice.

Later in the evening, Amanda said she'd accept the award, and Emil again prompted her to mention his role in the creation of *Star Roses*.

"Just think, we'll both be published authors. Just what we always dream about," said Emil, attempting to wrap his arm around Amanda's waist as she moved away.

✂

On May twenty-first, they flew to Vancouver for the awards ceremony. Since Amanda's discovery of her boyfriend's ruse and her reluctant agreement to accept the award, she had been more reticent than usual. But Emil felt she was coming around to his point of view, and he eagerly awaited the recognition that might pave the way for his new manuscript.

At the pre-awards ceremony, Amanda was warmly engaged with Lyle Carson. Emil had tried to insinuate himself into their conversation, and he felt neglected when their discussion quickly returned to Amanda's new manuscript.

"Well, we're delighted to forge a partnership with you, Amanda. You're certainly someone who fits well with what we do. *Star Roses* was just the start of a long and productive career for you," said Carson, casting an obligatory glimpse at Emil, as they filed into the auditorium for the awards presentation.

"Don't forget to give me a little plug, honey. We're in this together so may as well make the most of it, right?" urged Emil as the program's host introduced the recipient of the Canadian First Book Award.

Amanda climbed the steps to the stage and took her place at the podium. Emil applauded enthusiastically, prepared for his moment in the limelight. *Payback time,* he thought, his heart racing. What he heard greatly exceeded his expectations.

"Thank you so much for this wonderful acknowledgment," said Amanda, appreciatively. "It was a lot of hard work, but it was worth all those long days and nights toiling alone at the keyboard. I can't begin to express how I feel about this singular honor."

And with that, Amanda returned to her seat.

The one next to hers that had been occupied by Emil was now vacant. The award-winning author smiled wanly and placed the trophy in the empty chair.

About the Author

Michael C. Keith is the author of over twenty books on electronic media, among them *Talking Radio, Voices in the Purple Haze, Radio Cultures, Signals in the Air,* and the classic textbook *The Radio Station.* The recipient of numerous awards in his academic field, he is also the author of dozens of journal articles and short stories and has served in a variety of editorial positions. In addition, he is the author of an acclaimed memoir—*The Next Better Place,* a young adult novel—*Life is Falling Sideways,* and four story anthologies—*Of Night and Light, And Through the Trembling Air, Sad Boy,* and *Hoag's Object.* He has been nominated for a Pushcart Prize and Pen/O.Henry Award and was a finalist for the National Indie Excellence Award for short fiction anthology.